"I came straight f

Cassie continued, "What are you doing here?"
She forbade herself a glance toward the car.
Van would have to know sometime, but please
God, not now. Not yet.

"The house was a— We have to talk, Cass."

"What are you talking about?" She reached past
him for the knob. Just then, the back door of
her rental car opened, and a small voice called,
"Mommy?"

She turned and ran across the grass to snatch
her daughter into her arms, holding on so tight
Hope tried to wriggle free.

Van had followed, shock draining his face of
color.

Cassie shook her head, begging him not to say
anything that might hurt Hope. Naturally, he
wondered if she belonged to him. Despite five
years and the certainty he hadn't wanted her
or their marriage, Cassie feared answering his
unspoken question.

At last he dragged his gaze away from Hope,
moving his head as if his muscles were locked.

Cassie relented. "No. Not yours."

Dear Reader,

I was working on my previous book,
Temporary Father, when I realized Van Haddon,
a secondary character, had a richer life than I'd
understood. Van was a mainstay for his sister
and her son, but he was also hiding a secret love
that had no ending. After Van's wife, Cassie, was
attacked, she'd divorced him and begged him to
leave her alone for good—which left Van living
with the guilt that he hadn't loved her enough to
help her heal, when he would have given his life
to keep her safe.

Now Cassie's father is seriously ill, and Cassie's
bringing a secret home to Honesty—the daughter
who's given her life meaning. After her attack, she
left because she felt her father blamed her and Van
seemed repulsed by her. Back in Honesty, she finds
love can forgive.

But will her forgiveness extend to Van, who feels
he did Cassie and himself no favors by doing
things her way? He wants their life back. He just
has to persuade Cassie love's still worth having.

Let me know what you think of Honesty
and its busy citizens. You can reach me at
annaadamswriter.blogspot.com.

Best wishes,

Anna

THE MAN FROM HER PAST
Anna Adams

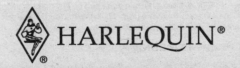

HARLEQUIN®

TORONTO • NEW YORK • LONDON
AMSTERDAM • PARIS • SYDNEY • HAMBURG
STOCKHOLM • ATHENS • TOKYO • MILAN • MADRID
PRAGUE • WARSAW • BUDAPEST • AUCKLAND

ISBN-13: 978-0-373-71435-3
ISBN-10:   0-373-71435-1

THE MAN FROM HER PAST

This edition published by arrangement with Harlequin Books S.A.

® and TM are trademarks of the publisher. Trademarks indicated with ® are registered in the United States Patent and Trademark Office, the Canadian Trade Marks Office and in other countries.

www.eHarlequin.com

Printed in U.S.A.

ABOUT THE AUTHOR

Anna Adams wrote her first romance in wet sand with a stick. The Atlantic Ocean washed that one away, so these days she uses more modern tools to write the kind of stories she loves best—romance that involves everyone in the family, and often the whole community. Love between two people is like the proverbial stone in a lake. The ripples of their feelings spread, bringing all kinds of conflict and "help" from the people who care most about them.

Anna is in the middle of one of those stories, with her own hero of twenty-seven years. From Iceland to Hawaii, and points in between, they've shared their lives with children and family and friends who've become family.

Books by Anna Adams

To Robert and Alice, and the love between you
that still makes the lives around you richer.

And to Uncle Cecil and Aunt Mary,
Aunt Dorothy and Aunt Bertha. Your strength
was mine. Your love kept me floating.
Your kindness heals my heart. Thank you
will never be enough, but if love counts—
well, I sure do love you all, my "other parents."

CHAPTER ONE

THUNDER CREPT across the sky, building strength to rattle Van Haddon's house. Rain and wind slapped at him so hard he hunched over as he climbed the wooden porch steps at the end of yet another business trip.

He used to love his job. For the past eleven months, he'd traveled at the drop of a hat, met with any financial client who seemed likely to sign on with him and all but begged for new business.

Getting into his house wasn't easy. He found the lock, despite the darkness of a storm-induced blackout, but another crack of thunder broke over his head. He jerked his hand, and the key came back out.

Faintly, he heard the telephone's insistent ring.

Van wiped rain off his face and tried again to get inside. Lightning flashed on the lock. He twisted the key and then kicked the front door open, shoving his carry-on out of the way as he grabbed the phone off a hall table. "Hello?"

"Van, Tom Drake here." The other man didn't have to add that he was the sheriff. Everyone who lived in the small town of Honesty, Virginia, knew who the sheriff was.

Van shouldered the door shut. "What's up, Tom?" He kept his tone carefully neutral. After two days of explaining a portfolio to a possible client who'd decided not to invest with him, he'd been grateful for the powerful December winds that had given the plane a boost all the way from San Diego. But as soon as he'd landed, all hell had broken loose. The storm had boiled over, and he couldn't forget last spring's disastrous lightning strike that had burned down his sister's fishing lodge.

"Something wrong with Beth or her family?"

"Beth and Eli are fine. In fact, I even think her new husband's home this week. I'm calling about Leo Warne."

Static broke up the words between syllables, but at Leo's name, Van let go of the strap on his laptop bag. It slid down his arm. He caught it and set the bag on the floor, shrugging out of his soaked coat at the same time.

"Leo?" He'd been Van's mentor, then his father-in-law and finally a walking wake-up call to his conscience.

"He's out here on the Mecklin Road Bridge. And I do mean *out* here. Half-dressed in a ratty shirt and boxers, cowering against the guardrail, scared out of his wits. He won't let us help him."

"Help him what?" Van loosened his tie and undid his top collar button. Five years ago, his ex-wife, Cassie, had left town, warning both her father and Van not to contact her again. Leo had soon suggested Van stay away from him, too.

They'd last seen each other a year ago in the canned vegetable aisle at Elljay's Market. One glance and they'd gone their separate ways.

Only family could be so cruel.

"I'm having no luck talking him into an ambulance," Tom said. "He's asking for his wife. He called me a liar when I said she was dead."

"I don't understand." Victoria had died while being treated for pneumonia when Cassie was fifteen.

"It's his mind, his memory. Something's wrong. He hasn't asked for Cassie, but he finally remembered you. I tried to make him see you'd want us to help him, but he won't move unless you come."

"Me?" Shock spotlighted the small things around him. Mail that had piled up. A picture of his nephew on a skateboard in midair. An unfolded, overdue bill for the credit card he used for travel expenses.

But he couldn't see Leo—always in charge, dressed to the extremes of elegance—scared and

nearly naked on a bridge in a storm that could literally kill him.

At seventy-three, Leo had retired as president
of Honesty Bank & Trust soon after Cassie had
left. Ashamed of what had happened to her, he'd
disappeared from the town's life.

Van couldn't explain anyone else's reasons,
but he had let Leo go because he'd hated the other
man's shame.

"Hell." He couldn't go on resenting Leo when
he needed help. Van checked his pockets for his
cell phone. "I'm on my way."

"Hurry. I'm afraid he'll jump."

Thunder jolted the house. A keening scream—
unbearable and hardly recognizable as Leo's
voice—seemed to form inside Van's head. "Take
my cell number in case you need it." He gave it
to Tom and then hung up.

Without a coat, without locking the door, with
nothing except fear that Leo had gone insane, Van
ran back into the storm.

He jumped into the car, switched on the
engine and jammed the gas pedal. All the way
down the driveway, the trees bent low, their
branches open hands grasping at his roof. He
skidded onto the main road.

How could he talk Leo off that bridge?

A truck crossed into his lane. Swearing, Van
swerved around it.

Someone had to tell Cassie.

Someone.

Who was he kidding? He'd have to tell Cassie.
Never mind that she'd long since stopped caring
enough to even hate him.

The attack had done that to them. Attack. That
was one way to put it—a way that let him face
himself. He'd been away on business. She'd been
home alone, and she'd left the bathroom window
open, no more than half an inch, to air out the steam.

Half an inch.

He hit the steering wheel with his fist. Half an
inch of air had changed Cassie forever, had forced
a space like thousands of miles between them.

He'd tried to reach her, but she'd shut him out,
lumping him with her father, who'd avoided her
after that night. After she'd gone, Van had wanted
to resent her, but he couldn't lie to himself. He'd
owed her more than just love.

Blue lights slashed the sky. Van slowed as he
neared the bridge. Clouds ambushed the moon
and swallowed its reflection. Blinking red bulbs
beneath the bridge flashed a warning to shipping
on the river. Behind Van, an 18-wheeler drew
close enough to illuminate the men milling in
front of the emergency vehicles.

Van parked behind a fire-and-rescue truck. As
he parted the crowd with his hands, rain poured
down his face, and lightning made him flinch.

"Leo?" He searched for the other man, yelling his name. Why hadn't someone in this thicket of blue-and-yellow-coated rescue workers scooped Leo up and run him to the hospital?

At last Van saw Tom. Four paramedics flanked the sheriff, two on each side. They all turned. Trey Lockwood, a longtime family friend, lifted his hand toward Van. Behind Trey, about thirty feet onto the bridge, Van glimpsed Leo's grizzled, frightened face above bony knees tucked close against his chest.

Sick to his stomach, Van shoved past the other men, but Tom took his arm. "Every time we try to get near him he backs out of reach, or we'd have grabbed him. He could stand up and jump at any moment."

"I'll get him." If he had to dive into that dark water in Leo's wake, he wasn't about to tell Cassie he'd let her father die.

"He may not know you." Tom had to yell over the weather and the noise of men and idling engines.

Van shook his head. "Does it matter? If we don't get him off this bridge, he'll die, anyway."

"Somebody get this man a coat," Tom said.

If he waited for a jacket, he might just end up wearing it to a funeral. "Leo." Edging closer, he left the knot of rescuers behind. His hands shook. He tried to look as if he were offering help, but he'd just as happily jerk the other man to safety.

"Go away." Leo turned his face toward the concrete guard rail.

"I can't." He'd been doing that for five years, and he was lucky Leo hadn't died. "We're still family. We were friends before Cassie and I even looked at each other."

"She loved you from day one."

She'd stopped easily enough. Van reached for the bridge railing, distracting Leo because it was easy to make the sick man follow his hand. Rain and wind gusted around them. Water rushed past the bridge supports below, but the voices behind them had quieted.

"Cassie's my little girl. Victoria will take care of her."

Van reached for the back of his collar as if something had slithered down his spine. It was one thing to hear Leo was sick, but another to see it.

So he lied. Anything to get his friend off this bridge. "Let me take you to them."

"I remember." Leo's hoarse voice suggested a sore throat and congestion. He pressed his fists into his eyes.

"Let me help."

"I don't want to remember."

"Just remember me long enough to trust me."

Leo lifted eyes that refused to focus. "You look funny. Not like you used to."

Five years of loneliness changed any man. "I'm older."

"Older?" His voice trailed off as if he didn't understand the word. He leaned harder against the bridge. "Bring me Victoria." Her name, something familiar, comforted him. "*You* can't help."

"I can't get Victoria."

"I'm not the one who's crazy here." Bracing his hand on the concrete, drawing himself up on one knee, Leo resurrected a semblance of his old dignity. "She's not dead."

He pointed at a paramedic on Tom's left. "Like he said. Wouldn't I know?" With a bone-shaking cough, he sank back to the pavement, his legs folding like matchsticks.

Van hurried at least five feet closer.

"Victoria..." Leo's gasp was desperate. "She'd never leave." He jabbed the air in front of Van, his bent finger shaking. "You find her. Now."

"You're freezing and sick, and this rain is making you worse."

"Get away from me." He waved a wasted arm.

"You taught me my job. You probably taught me how to be a man. You would have been my best friend all my life." Only vaguely aware of the men behind them, he didn't care what they thought. "You were like my father once. Let me walk you off this bridge."

"I'm not sick." The bones in his scrawny throat

moved up and down. "You'll drag me straight to the hospital, and people die there. I've seen it." He frowned in confusion.

He had to mean Victoria, but maybe the memory was too painful to face. "Aren't you hungry?" Van prayed Leo's weight loss came from forgetting about mealtimes, rather than a serious illness. "Let's get something to eat, a hot drink. We'll talk all night, the way we used to."

Leo shook his head. His mouth moved, but no sound came out.

Van took a chance and moved in, slipping a hand beneath the other man's arm. God, his bones. "Come with me. We'll find you a coat and some food."

Awareness slowly lit Leo's dull expression. His chin dipped to his chest. "Don't tell Cassie. She doesn't speak to me." He lowered his voice. Van had to bend all the way down to hear. "Not in years."

Van patted his arm, the way he would a child's. "She doesn't talk to me, either, but I'll call her tonight. I'll make her listen."

"She hates me."

"You're wrong about that. She'll tell you." He couldn't meet Leo's eyes. Who knew how Cassie felt about either of them? "Come sit in my car."

"I don't have to sit in one of those trucks? I hate those lights. They get inside my head." He pressed his hands to his wet hair, trying to squeeze out the strobing flashes.

Van looked to the paramedics, who were inching closer, coiled to spring. No one offered advice. Could Leo be reacting to medication? Was that wishful thinking? If only he'd been around enough to know.

"The lights bother me, too, but my car's pretty dark. See if you feel better there."

Leo got halfway to his feet, but as Van was on the verge of shouting with relief, the older man collapsed against him. "Don't let me die in that hospital."

Van tried again to help him stand. "What happened to Victoria was a fluke. You know most people get help in a hospital. And you need help." He refused to let Leo brush his hands away.

"They'll kill me. I know."

"I'll go with you." Van made a production of wiping his nose. "I'm not feeling too great, either."

Leo squinted through the rain soaking his face. "Are you sick, too?"

"I think so." He'd rarely felt more torn up. He'd given Cassie the divorce she'd demanded and gone meekly away as she'd asked. He'd lost track of her father, and he couldn't find his old friend in this shell of a man. "How about if we both go with these guys?" He pointed at the EMTs. "They'll check us out on the way."

He coughed, feeling ludicrous, but Leo let him help him all the way up. "I'm freezing," Van said.

"I might be a little cold, too."

They shuffled, arms around each other, toward the ambulance. The paramedics closed in on Leo, seized his arms and began moving him at rapid speed. He searched over his shoulder for Van, desperation naked on his face.

Van wiped his eyes and then checked to make sure no one else had noticed. He and Leo had been close since he'd first marched into the bank to ask for an internship. He trotted to catch up. "Can I ride along?" he asked the nearest EMT, who turned out to be Trey.

"Sure, if it'll ease Mr. Warne's mind."

"You need to check him, too," Leo said.

The other guy looked at Van, who shook his head slightly.

The ambulance distracted Leo. He climbed onto it, slowly taking in the noise and machines. One of his rescuers eased him onto a stretcher. Immediately, the driver got in the front, and Trey and another EMT started treating Leo.

Van sat out of the way on the opposite side of the ambulance. Trey and his partner contacted the hospital, started an IV, and reported Leo's symptoms and vitals.

From between the two men, Leo's hand suddenly jutted out, splayed like a frightened child's. Van caught it and folded the gnarled, trembling fingers into his palm.

IN THE KIND HEART woman's shelter in Tecumseh, Washington, Cassie Warne was carrying a tray of cookies and milk to her office to share with her daughter when a man crashed through the locked double doors behind her in a hail of splinters and broken wood.

Cassie turned, transfixed by chunks of the door clattering at her feet. At first she thought the man was brandishing a baseball bat, but it was a metal battering ram.

He snarled a name Cassie couldn't hear. She didn't ask him to repeat it. Women and children going about the business of getting settled for the night, froze. The man searched them for the one he wanted, and Cassie's instinct took over.

She never let herself dwell on that night five years ago. It had happened, like her mother's death, and her broken arm on her eleventh birthday. It was only a fact, but it had changed her.

She needed no one and no one would ever hurt her or anyone who depended on her.

The tray slipped from her hands. The plate and glasses smashed. Vaguely aware of glass shards on the floor among the bits of broken wood, she felt time jerk to a start again.

Cassie threw herself at the man, praying her

four-year-old daughter would stay in the office, out of sight.

Silently, she swung the edge of her foot into the man's belly. Though her own stomach heaved, she never looked away from his eyes. She'd seen rage like that—uninhibited, unstinting fury in a face looming over her one night when Van had been in D.C. or Milwaukee or Fresno. Somewhere other than their tiny apartment bedroom.

With a cartoon "oof," the man backed away, doubling over. His battering ram fell to the floor and scattered the wood and glass.

Please, she thought, let him stop now. Don't make me do anything else.

He straightened with a feral snarl.

Crying because she didn't want to do it, Cassie pointed her elbow into his throat. Her martial arts instructors had taught her to yell, supposedly to strike fear into an attacker and bolster her strength. She needed nothing but the will to hurt another human being. Still she felt sick as the man began to choke.

And damn him. He kept coming.

She was crying as the heel of her palm rammed his nose into his skull. Blood on her hands gagged her as he dropped, unconscious.

She hovered, ready, trembling from head to toe.

"Mommy?"

"Hope."

Cassie turned, gathering herself as if she'd also been broken into pieces. She rubbed her arm across her eyes and her mouth, trying to erase any trace of the violence that had adrenaline bubbling in her veins.

Gripping the office door, Hope pointed at Cassie's shirt. A scream poured out of her throat.

Cassie looked down. The blood snapped her straight back to reality.

"I'm okay." She tore the shirt off. "I'm all right, baby."

Hope rushed her. Cassie knelt and scooped her daughter into her arms. "The police," she said to the nearest woman. She threw her shirt far away. In her bra and jeans, she was wearing more than some of the clients who'd shown up at their doors.

She cuddled Hope, keeping her as safe as she could from scary things. "We're all okay, baby." To herself, she sounded calm while her heartbeat shook her whole body. In a few minutes, Hope's crying faded to a whimper.

"Wanna go home, Mommy. Bad, bad man." As she pointed at him with a four-year-old's contempt, sirens sounded.

"Put this on." Liza, one of Cassie's partners, dropped a faded Tecumseh PD T-shirt over Cassie's shoulder. Another woman must have worn it into the shelter. Cassie pulled it over her head, and Hope helped her yank it down.

"You hurt that bad man, Mommy."

"I know." She seriously wanted to bury her head. "It was scary."

"I'm glad you hurt him."

She didn't know what to say. Normally, *it's not nice to hit people* would do, but the man had come bent on hurting someone in the shelter. She couldn't let that happen.

Cassie cradled Hope's chin. Violence had changed Cassie's life forever, and she'd tried to make sure the past wasn't part of her present with Hope. "I don't like hurting anyone, baby, but that man wanted to be mean to someone here." Of their own volition, her thoughts returned to that other bad man, and she hated the fear that whispered through her in a warning.

Unconditional love looked out of Hope's blue eyes.

"I won't ever scare you if I can help it," Cassie said. Her daughter meant everything to her.

"You didn't look like my mommy."

Cassie hugged her tight. Someday she'd teach Hope the self-defense she'd made every shelter employee learn, but she didn't want her daughter to think of her as a woman who beat people up.

She went blank when she tried to think what else she should have done.

Two policemen, guns drawn, barged through the splintered doorway and stopped in front of the unconscious man.

Only then did Cassie realize one woman had picked up his battering ram and another stood over him with a raised chair.

More concerned about the guns, she turned Hope's face into her chest.

"Danger's over." Liza pointed at his revolver. "You can put that away. We don't like the children to see them."

The police both holstered their weapons. "What happened?" asked the one she'd spoken to.

"He busted in with this." She eased the battering ram out of the woman's hand. "And my friend stopped him from getting any further."

"Which friend?" the second cop asked.

Cassie stood, lifting Hope onto her hip. "He said someone's name, but I didn't catch it." She searched the suspicious glances of the women and children around them. "Anyone know him?"

"I do," the second cop said. "He's a fireman. I can't remember his name, but we worked together last year when the county put on that disaster training."

No one else claimed him.

The downed man began to stir and the first policeman cuffed him. He nodded at Cassie. "He wasn't looking for you?"

Shaking her head, she hugged Hope closer. "I work here."

"She's a partner," Liza said. "I'm Liza Crane. This is Cassie Warne. We have another partner, Kim Fontaine, but she works day hours."

So did Cassie, but Hope had been out of school for a teacher in-service day. For the first time in Hope's short preschool career, Cassie had forgotten to arrange for backup day care.

Between them, the police officers dragged the man to his feet. Catching sight of Cassie, he lunged.

"Bitch."

She backed up, turning Hope away from him.

"Bad man." Her daughter burrowed her face into Cassie's shirt.

WITH A TRACE of leftover nerves-on-alert, Cassie hurried Hope into their town house four hours later. She locked the door and shut out the world. Her haven of overstuffed chairs and verdant plants and overflowing bookshelves let her breathe again.

She sought the familiar. Prints from museums she'd visited when she could only stare at walls and pray not to scream. Framed pieces of Hope's artwork, going all the way from scrawls and handprints to the big faces with stringy hands and feet she favored lately.

"No bad men here." Hope slid from Cassie's arms and ran to her room, all order restored in her world.

Cassie breathed easier. The event had only scared Hope for a little while. It hadn't changed her life.

Setting the dead bolt on the front door, Cassie activated the alarm system. "Are you hungry?"

"Can we have eggs and cheese? All stirred up together?"

"Perfect." Comfort food.

Cassie went to the kitchen. Hope skipped in while she was pulling the mixing bowl out of a cabinet.

"Wait for me, Mommy. You know I'm 'posed to help."

"It wouldn't taste the same without you."

Cassie broke eggs into a bowl. Hope whisked them all over the kitchen counter and the sink, and Cassie mixed up chocolate milk. They toasted each other while a golden pat of butter sizzled in the iron skillet Cassie had taken from her childhood home.

"That man doesn't know where we live?"

Cassie shook her head. "And the police won't let him out, anyway."

Hope set her glass on the counter and then wrapped her arms around Cassie's thighs. Cassie leaned down and hugged her tight. And that seemed to be the end of it all.

"I'll get that peach stuff Mrs. Kleiber made me." Hope hurried to the fridge for a jar of preserves their neighbor made for her every year.

Cassie dropped bread into the toaster slots, grateful for Hope's resilience. "How hungry are we after such a long day?"

The phone cut into Hope's answer. As Cassie lifted the receiver, she saw that their machine had recorded eleven messages. Without bothering to look at the caller ID, she said hello.

"Cassie?"

That voice. Low, more uncertain than she'd ever heard it, but rich and familiar as his touch had once been. She shivered as memories of his hands on her body made her ache, arms and legs, heart and soul.

In a night of shocks, this one made her grab the edge of the counter.

"Van?" She'd read in romances that a man could make a woman light-headed enough to faint. But those women had been bound in Jane Austen finery. She was still sporting splinter-laden jeans and a Tecumseh PD T-shirt. "Van."

She'd loved him. She couldn't remember a time when she hadn't, but she'd had to leave him because he couldn't love her after she'd been raped.

CHAPTER TWO

"MOMMY?"

She shook her head at Hope, urging the girl she loved more than her own life to keep quiet.

"What's wrong?" Cassie couldn't control the huskiness in her voice. Hope stared. Cassie cleared her throat. Van shouldn't matter this much after five years. "How did you get my number?"

"From your father."

Her heart tap-danced. Something must be horribly wrong. "Why are you calling?"

"It's your dad," he said. "The cops and paramedics found him on the Mecklin Road Bridge. He didn't recognize them. He called for your mother." He waited, as if to let it sink in.

It did with a thud. "He didn't know she was dead?"

"Eventually he remembered." Maybe Van kept stopping because he didn't know what to say. *She* didn't know what to say. Of all the scenarios she'd imagined drawing her home, this was the one she really hadn't wanted to face. "I'm sorry," Van said.

"How bad is he?" Her grandmother had died after battling Alzheimer's disease. Her father had deeply feared a similar fate. "Is this a one-night problem, or could it be my grandmother's illness?"

"I don't know." Van's weariness scared her more than his words.

"Mommy?"

"Everything's all right." Straightening, she yanked the frying pan off the burner and spoke firmly, to comfort her child and to keep Van from guessing she was talking to a little one.

Hope, who'd been through too much, misunderstood and ran to her room. Cassie followed her into the hall. She couldn't explain Van to Hope or her to him.

"I have to come home." She'd been raised by a loving mother and a responsible father who'd taught her to think of others. Rarely had she been selfish in her life—not because she was noble, but because her parents had never accepted such behavior. But—home?

She'd dreaded this day for five years, had felt it threatening like a bag of bricks hanging over her head.

She pulled herself together. "I'm coming."

"I can take care of him." Van stopped again.

"How?" she asked. "You're not his next of kin. You're not even family anymore."

His breathing deepened. How could she possibly hurt him after all this time?

"I'm sorry," she said.

"No, you're right. It was crazy to offer. Not long after you left, he also told me to stay away. But I thought maybe that was an excuse I was happy to take."

"I don't want to know—" It was too late to catch up on what had happened after she'd left. The time they'd shared had belonged to someone else. It didn't feel like hers any longer. "I'll be on my way as soon as I can get a flight."

"Wait, Cassie. Let me pick you up at the airport."

So she could explain Hope at baggage claim? Not a chance. "I'll be fine."

His silence ran thick, full of words unsaid. Their relationship had ended unnaturally when she'd walked away, but she hadn't been willing to wait for the usual recriminations and anger. The rape had humiliated Van and her father. She'd hated them both until she realized she'd never love Hope while she nourished bitterness.

"Thank you for calling," she said, "and for helping my father. I'll take over as soon as I get there, and you can go back to your own life."

"I'm trying to warn you he isn't the same." He didn't seem to hear anything she said, as if he had an agenda and was checking off the items. "I don't think he's been eating, and I don't know when he last took a shower."

"That's not my dad." An image of him burned in her mind. "They'll keep him in the hospital until I get there?"

"I doubt they'd let him out. When should I expect you?"

"As soon as I can make a reservation. Your number must be on my phone. I'll call you back."

"Let me give it to you to make sure."

She wrote it down. "Thank you," she said.

"Cassie?"

She bit her lip. Hard. Her arms and legs felt heavy, strange. As if she were channeling someone else's feelings. If only Van would stop saying her name. "What?"

"Are you all right?"

He'd always cared. That had never been the problem, but his concern left her empty now. "Fine."

A few seconds went by. She should hang up, cut off the thick voice that had haunted her dreams a lot longer than the monster's who'd broken into their bathroom. The monster's voice only terrified her.

Van's made her lonely, reminded her how it felt to be intimate. Not sex, but trust and talk and safety.

"Should I get you a room at the hotel?" he asked.

She wasn't about to put Hope on display for the kind, but too-quick-to-pity citizens of Honesty. "I'll stay at Dad's house."

"Maybe you'd like to try Beth's fishing lodge? She had some trouble last year, but the place is up and running again. She got married last summer and she and her husband renovated—"

Running on wasn't like him. "I'll stay at home." She'd had to give up Beth's unstinting friendship, and it was too late to start over or explain.

"Okay." His tone tightened. "Don't forget to let me know when you'll be here."

For the first time since high school, he didn't say *I love you* as he hung up. Even the last time— months after she'd left, while Hope had kicked lazily in her belly and Van had begged for another chance, and she'd asked him to stop calling, he'd said it.

She clicked the off button, sliding her palms over her face as if to wipe away memories of Van that flew at her. Always laughing—as she ran her hands through his silky dark blond hair. As he took her mouth with his. Laughter dying as he moved his body above hers.

She flinched and grabbed the wall. "Hope?" After a deep breath, she hurried to her daughter's room. "I have to tell you some things."

"No, Mommy. I'm mad. You talked mean to me."

"I'm sorry, honey." She was so careful. She tried never to raise her voice, never to let Hope see a hint of brutality anywhere. Her stomach lurched as she remembered the softness of the intruder's body this afternoon. The human body was so fragile.

And the psyche more so.

"Who was on the phone?" Hope asked, with eyes only for her doll.

"A man I used to know—a friend of my father's."

"Huh?" Hope's eyes rounded and she dropped the doll on her pink-flowered comforter. "You have a daddy?"

Cassie tilted her head back. She'd never even mentioned him? "I have a father," she said. "He's sick and he needs me to look after him."

"Like when I'm sick?" Hope grabbed her hand. "Ooh, will we make him glasses of ice water and toast?"

"We can make anything that will help him feel better. Let's talk about it over our eggs. Help me warm them up?"

"VAN, TAKE THESE KEYS." Frail in his hospital gown, Leo Warne covered them with his hand, like a spy passing off a top secret microfiche. "They're not safe here. Someone will steal them and break into the house and clean me out." Leo's eyes darted toward the door and back.

Van suppressed a shudder. He'd loved the man like a father. How could he have abandoned him? "Don't worry. Cassie's going to stay at the house. Your stuff will be safe."

"Stop looking at me like I'm a stranger. I'm not sick." He nodded toward the ceiling as if someone were watching them from above. "I'm just a smart old man. Something no one in this town likes. I know how they treated Cassie. They made her leave, looking down on her after that man…" He swallowed, his Adam's apple as big as an egg in his too-thin throat. "Like the rape was her fault. No one took care of her." He skewered Van with blue eyes that were so much like Cassie's. "Not even you."

Van gripped the edge of Leo's rolling tray. "The rape repulsed me. Cassie never did. I should have protected her, but I couldn't even make her see I still loved her."

"Because you didn't. I know. I know it all. I walk around this town in the night. No one sees me. I'm invisible."

Van stared, his own good sense returning. "You're tired and sick and you need to be cared for." Van dared to stroke Leo's thin hair as he would have touched his own father—or his child, if he and Cassie had been so lucky. "You'll get better and you'll start remembering."

"I remember everything. People laughed at her

and they said she deserved it. They said she should have been more careful. She was asking for it."

"Those are your own fears talking. It never happened."

"It was worse. You don't even know. She won't come home now."

"She'll be here tomorrow. She's planning to stay at your house."

The house. With his heart breaking for his broken friend, he felt anxious. What would Cassie walk into in her childhood home? If Leo hadn't washed himself in weeks, he certainly hadn't cleaned the house.

Cassie had enough to face. No one had understood why she'd run away from Honesty. Her former neighbors would flood her with casseroles. They'd sympathize with her about Leo's illness and they'd fish for answers about why she'd stayed away so long.

They'd tried often enough to extract the truth from Van, but no one seemed to realize she hadn't been content to cut the town out of her life. She'd had no more room for her father or her ex-husband, either.

"Leo, I'm heading over to your house for a while. Just to make sure everything's ready for Cassie."

"I'll give you a buck and a half to mow the

lawn." Leo dug for a nonexistent pocket. "It's not worth that much, but I know you. You'll just spend it on a Coca-Cola with Cassie, and you shouldn't be paying for her treats."

Van felt as if he'd run face first into a wall, but Leo didn't seem to realize it was December. "Pay me later." Van wondered which lawn guy had flirted with Cassie. Van hadn't noticed her as more than a cute kid until after he'd been working in the bank for almost a year and she'd started college.

He pushed his fist against his chest. They'd been a family once, the three of them. He kissed his former father-in-law's head and hurried out.

At the nurses' station, he backed up and asked them to call if Leo's condition changed. Despite all signs to the contrary, he hoped Leo might improve before Cassie arrived. Good food, warmth and attentive care had to give him a chance.

The Warnes lived across the lake from Beth's fishing lodge. Van pulled up to Leo's place to find Trey Lockwood, one of last night's EMTs, banging away at the front porch with a hammer. Trey stopped and brushed back his ball cap with a weary sigh. He pulled a couple of nails from between his lips.

"I didn't expect to find anyone else here," Van said. "What's wrong with the porch?"

Trey stepped on a board and it squeaked. "Ann and I didn't realize we should have checked on him."

"Has he been acting odd for long?"

"He definitely changed after Cassie…" He didn't say the words and Van was just as glad. "We thought you probably knew, but you weren't welcome here, either."

"I'd have forced my way in." He took in the paint peeling off the siding. Why hadn't he driven past once in a while? The answer would keep him from facing himself in a mirror for a while. He'd been a coward. Pretending Leo and Cassie didn't matter anymore had been easier than fighting them for a few pathetic minutes of their time.

"You look gutted," Trey said. "People think everyone knows what goes on in small towns. But the doors shut here, just like anywhere else, and some things you can't know."

Trey was a smart guy. "The door didn't shut on this." Van pulled Leo's keys out of his jacket pocket. "I'll see how things look inside."

"Yeah. Good luck. Let me know if I can help."

"Thanks." Van trod the rickety boards with care. He dreaded opening the door. "Cassie's due back tomorrow."

"You don't want her to see what's been going on with her dad."

"I can't protect her from what's happened to her father, but I'd like to clean this place a little."

"She shouldn't have left." Even after five years, Van turned to defend Cassie, but Trey tested the next step, looking regretful. He'd been Cassie's friend, too. He yanked and the plank gave way with a scream. "None of us asked her to go. None of us wanted her to."

"It was my fault," Van said, surprising himself. "Not hers." A floorboard groaned as he eased across it. A strong wind could send the porch across the lake to Beth's yard. "It's too late to talk about the past," he said.

"You gotta talk to someone." Trey held a nail against the board and hammered. "Sometime." He added another nail. "Or it'll drive you crazy."

"Yeah?" Van turned the key in the lock, but it took determination, as if Leo hadn't locked it in five years. He looked over his shoulder at the lake. Leo rented a boathouse down there, hidden by the pines. Three years ago, Van had discovered it open, and he'd locked it to keep it safe from vandals. He'd left a note, telling Leo to get in touch with him for the lock's combination, but Leo had never called about it.

Trey was watching. "I'll finish out here. I know a guy who can repaint fast. Cassie'll feel at home."

Van nodded. "Thanks for the help and the therapy."

The EMT grinned. "Free of charge, buddy."

He went back to work, and Van turned the doorknob and shoved it open. The hinges screamed for oil. A stench of decay and dirt almost knocked him back down the steps.

"God." He stared at newspapers and canned goods stacked in ranks like soldiers waiting to march down the hall. On each tread of the staircase along the right wall, three packages of paper towels stood side by side.

He pushed the door wide and went searching for the source of the smell. It was easy to trace it to the dining room.

Food. Old, old food, and food as new as last night's dinner.

He slammed his hand over his mouth like any heroine in one of the old movies his sister loved to watch. Apparently, Leo had thought getting the food to the dining room was enough. There were china plates on the table, but at some point he'd switched to paper and plastic utensils.

And then he'd stopped washing dishes. He'd neatly aligned the plates and the cups and glassware and, eventually, he'd done the same with the throwaway stuff, unless he hadn't finished his meal. Those plates perched on any surface—and the floor.

Compulsive neatness and haphazard filth. How had it made sense?

The kitchen was even crazier. Completely spotless, except there wasn't a dish to be found, beyond the paper and plastic in the cabinets where the real stuff used to be stored.

"Dear God, Leo."

In the back of his mind, Van had blamed Leo for Cassie's leaving. If her beloved father hadn't been ashamed, maybe Cassie would have given Van another chance, but Leo's humiliation had blinded her. She'd taken Van's revulsion at his inability to help her, for shame like her father's.

He choked in a breath and grabbed a garbage bag from beneath the sink. He set to work, realizing he'd misread Leo. They'd tried to live with their guilt in different ways.

He'd been unable to touch his wife, and Leo had stopped living in a world that made sense.

"HOW MUCH LONGER, Mommy?" From her car seat in the back of their rental, Hope flipped her cloth doll, Penny, in circles until the arms coiled like springs. "Where is my grampa, anyway?"

"In a hospital, honey." Squinting into the fading evening sun, Cassie passed another highway sign that assured her she was on her way to Honesty, Virginia. She didn't need the sign. She knew each bump and dip of the road like the corners of her childhood bedroom.

"Will he like me?"

"You're funny. How could anyone not love you?" It was what Cassie feared. It was the reason she'd told no one back home that she'd had Hope. The reason she'd never returned.

"He didn't come see me. We never visited him in his neighborgood."

They'd recently started looking for a new house in a "neighborhood with a great school." Hope couldn't get the hang of the word.

"He's an older man."

"Mrs. Bonney is a older lady." She usually babysat when Cassie had to work late. She made cookies and crocheted afghans and loved Hope almost as much as Cassie did. "She wants to see me all the time."

"But she lives right next door."

"She goes away. She goes to see her little girls."

Mrs. Bonney called her granddaughters her little girls.

Cassie searched for answers. She'd told her father to stay away. She couldn't explain why. "Mrs. Bonney isn't sick."

"Is my grampa a nice man?"

A simple yes stuck in her throat. He'd blamed her for the rape. And he hadn't loved her since.

Van, too. Van, who'd been so much her other half that excising him had left gaps in her soul. Maybe he was worse than her father, because he'd vowed to be her husband. Better or worse had broken him.

"I'm talking to you, Mommy."

"I told you all this last night, sweetie, but you might not get to see him, since he's in the hospital."

"I thought we were gonna get him out of there."

"It's not a bad place." Another hint she should look at her current work situation. So many of the women at the shelter went to the hospital, and their husbands were kept from seeing them. From phone calls Hope had overheard, and frankness about work that Cassie and her partners should have forgone, she might have gotten the wrong idea.

"I don't want to go."

"You don't have to." Cassie's stomach dropped. Who'd look after Hope while she was with her father? How many people in Honesty would have to see Hope? "We're not staying here long," Cassie said.

"But how long?"

"A few days."

She could hear her old friends.

When did she have that kid?

Why didn't she tell Van?

Whose kid is that?

Van would wonder why she'd hidden Hope's existence.

"You don't have to explain." Her counselor in Tecumseh had repeated that over and over in the months after Hope was born. "She's your responsibility. You have to make a good life for her and you. And frankly, to hell with anyone else."

Cassie's father, practically a Biblical patriarch in her mind when she was growing up, hadn't wanted her after she was tainted. He certainly wouldn't want Hope. When Cassie had needed him most, he'd blamed her for the worst thing that had ever happened to her.

She'd find help for him. She closed her burning eyes tight for a second. She'd provide medical care if he needed it. She owed him nothing more.

"Where's my gramma, Mommy?"

That question hadn't come up last night. "I'm sorry, but you don't have one," Cassie said, fighting, as always, the soft memory of her mother's hands on her face, her whispered reassurance that the dark was safe. "My mom died when I was a teenager."

Hope, who'd been traveling since early morning and missed her nap, looked as if she might cry. "You won't ever die, will you, Mommy?"

"Not for a long time, Hope." According to the policeman who'd taken her statement at the shelter, she had every chance of dying pretty soon if she wasn't more careful about taking on thugs. She'd tried to explain about the advantage of surprise. He hadn't been impressed, and he was right. He just hadn't come up with an alternative response, other than everyone hiding— and who could do that all the time?

"Good." Hope smiled through a soft veil of tears in her eyes. Blessed with a sensitive heart, she'd always cried easily. "But you don't have a mommy."

"I'm used to that." Who ever got used to that?

"It's a good thing you have me."

Cassie laughed. "Having you is the best. I love you this much." She took her hands off the wheel long enough to spread them as far as she could. "And then some."

"Good." Hope tucked her baby onto her shoulder. "I'm not sleepy, Mommy."

"I see that."

"But I could use some mac and cheese."

"Just let me know when. We'll be home before you know it." Home. She'd said it without thinking, after five years of dreading the sight of Honesty.

"We can make eggs for my grampa."

The hospital concept proved tricky for her to grasp. Cassie glanced in the rearview, at Hope's drooping eyelids.

With any luck, she could keep this trip an adventure for her daughter and then escape. No one who'd known Cassie before would see Hope, or ask questions.

HOPE WAS ASLEEP when Cassie parked in front of her father's home. With her palms sweating on the steering wheel, she stared at the house, low, squat and dingy in moonlight instead of the rich blue of her memory. The ivy her father had tended so lovingly had taken over the porch and the roof, trying to pull the house down.

A woman could almost wish it had.

She glanced at Hope, hating to wake her until she saw what awaited them inside. Van had said her father would still be in the hospital, but when had Leo Wainwright Warne ever paid attention to anyone or anything other than his own sense of right and wrong?

Wallowing in a hospital bed would strike him as the height of wrong.

Cassie climbed out of the car, eased the door shut and started up the cracked driveway. Then she stopped, eyeing the house and a dark band of cloth blocking off the porch. Someone had pinned a Wet Paint sign to it. She leaned down to touch a step. Tacky. And that wasn't all.

The ivy, cracks in the dirty cement, black tire streaks and bird droppings dotting the graying pavement. Her father hadn't been out here with his pressure washer in a long time.

Five years couldn't change anything this much—not unless time and neglect had lived hand in hand. Van had tried to warn her about her father. Like Hope, she just hadn't got it.

She went around to the kitchen door. Half expecting to find it unlocked, she nonetheless lifted her key.

Only to have the door open in her face and Van come out.

Without thinking, she turned toward the car. He took her arm as if to stop her from running. She looked down at his broad hand, his splayed, capable fingers.

Her body seemed to grow heavier, but she wasn't confused about her real feelings. She looked up at him and prayed Hope wouldn't wake, the way children did when a car stopped too long.

"I thought I'd be out of here before you arrived." Stress tensed his face. His dark green eyes watched her as if she were a stranger.

"You dreaded seeing me, too." She pulled away from him. How could he bother her so much after five years? After the revulsion he hadn't been able to hide before she'd left?

She started over.

"I came straight from the airport," she said. "What are you doing here?" She forbade herself another glance toward Hope. Sometime he'd have to know but, please God, not now. Not yet.

"The house was a—we have to talk, Cass."

"Don't call me that." Her old nickname tugged her toward him as if he were her true north. Everyone had used it, but from Van it meant familiarity and whispers in the cocoon of their bed. Secrets only they knew.

He nodded, his eyes so intense she wanted to scream. He shut the door behind him. "Parts of the house were in bad shape. Are in bad shape."

"What are you talking about?" She reached past him. Just then, the back door of her rental car opened, and a small voice shouted, "Mommy?"

She turned. "Hope." Cassie ran across the grass and snatched her daughter into her arms, holding on so tight Hope tried to wriggle free.

"You're squishing me."

"Sorry." Tears choked her, but she never cried. "Sorry, baby." She turned, her daughter in her arms.

Van had followed, shock draining his face of color. She wished the sunset would just finish up and fade and make them all invisible.

Cassie shook her head, begging him not to say anything that might hurt Hope. Naturally, he wondered if she belonged to him. Despite five years and the certainty he hadn't wanted her or their marriage, she feared his unspoken question.

At last, he dragged his gaze away from Hope, moving his head as if his muscles were locked. Pain pulsed from his body.

Cassie relented. She'd assumed a lot of bad things about Van's inability to be human, but he obviously had feelings.

"No," she said. "Not yours."

He grimaced, looking confused. Then he put his hand over his mouth. She was close enough to see sweat bead on his upper lip.

As it had the last time he'd tried to make love to her.

She'd been right to leave Honesty. She was the only one who could love the whimsical, curious girl who danced through her life in joy.

Only Cassie could love the daughter born of her rape.

CHAPTER THREE

"MOMMY, WHOZZAT MAN?"

Van's eyes darkened. His mouth froze in a sharp, thin line. He clenched his fists at his side.

Cassie pressed her face to her daughter's head and breathed in Hope's warm, still-babyish scent. Cassie swore silently. He could still make her tremble, but she and Hope were a family.

"Van, this is Hope, the love of my life." Be careful, she warned him in her head. Don't say anything to hurt my daughter. "Baby, this is Mr. Van. He's a—" She stopped. If explaining Hope's long-lost Grampa had been hard... "a friend of my father's."

"Hello, Mr. Van." Hope stuck out her tiny hand. As always, Cassie marveled at her long slender fingers. She'd know her daughter decades from now, if only by her hands. God had been kind. They were Victoria Warne's hands, too. "Mr. Van?" her little girl said.

He literally shook himself, staring at her.

"Is he okay?" Hope stage-whispered.

He forced a false smile, but Cassie was grateful. Finally, he dwarfed her hand in his and shook it.

Giggling, Hope dropped her head against Cassie's chest and didn't see Van press his palm to his jeans.

Watching him, Cassie felt more than the cold of the Virginia winter. Not even the coat she'd draped over the backseat would have warmed her. Why had she expected anything more compassionate from him?

"Sorry." He shook his head. His disgust this time was clearly for himself, but it came too late.

Cassie swept past him. "I'm taking her inside for dinner and bed."

"There's no food," he said, "and a couple of the rooms…"

She waited. He didn't go on. She didn't look back. "What about the rooms?"

"Your dad." He came after them. The kitchen steps dipped beneath his weight. "He had some collections."

"What are you trying to say?"

"Paper towels," he said. "And those dishwashing sponges. Hundreds of them."

"What?" She stared at him underneath the porch light.

"In the guest rooms. I've cleaned your room and his and your old playroom, and I cleaned off

and remade the daybed in there. But the others—
I called the women's shelter in town to see if they
could use anything."

He actually blushed, but for no valid reason.
Obviously, his mind had gone to the women's
shelter because of what had happened to her.
They'd be well sponged and paper-towel clean,
because she'd forgotten she'd left her bathroom
window open one night five years ago.

"Get over it, Van. I have."

"Have you?"

His simple question rattled all her doubts. "I
had to." She glanced down at Hope's head.

He wiped his mouth again. "I don't know how
to talk to you."

"Fortunately," she said, trying to be kind because
she didn't want grudges between them, "we don't
need to talk. Don't get me wrong. I'm grateful for
everything you've done. We'll both have beds to
sleep in, and I can go by the grocery store."

"Let me."

"We're not your problem. Good night."

"Come on, Cass." She'd known Van nearly all
her life, but never had she heard the kind of anger
he was fighting to quell—all the more frightening because he was normally so controlled. "Give
me a chance," he said. "What did you expect me
to do when I found out?"

She looked down. Hope's eyes had drifted

shut. "I expected the reaction you had. That's why I left town and never meant to come back."

"Not because you didn't love me anymore?"

She stopped, feeling naked, sensing the eyes of everyone who'd ever known her in this town. "You stopped loving me," she said, praying Hope was really asleep and not just pretending.

"I always told you I was the problem." He edged closer to her shoulder as if emotion brought him there. His nearness and her unaccountable urge to remember what it was like to be in his arms made her want to scream.

"I know. It's not you. It's me." Hearing Cassie's frustration, Hope tried to lift her head, but she was too tired. "Go home, Van. I'm busy."

"Let me help you carry your things in. The house will be a shock."

"I don't need your help." She opened the door. Something smelled awful, and the kitchen looked darker than she remembered.

Van stepped inside.

"Bad man," Hope muttered.

"Not overly bad." No doubt Hope would have to see him again. Cassie walked around him and tried to shut the door, but he wouldn't let her.

"I feel as if I'm barging in, but the house is going to come as a shock." The past, moments in time that should have ended, reopened the gulf between them.

"I'm fine."

Her little girl looked up. "Mommy, what are you talking about?"

"Old stuff," Cassie said. "And what you and I should have for dinner. Can you stay awake long enough to eat something?"

"I'm pretty hungry."

"Me, too."

Hope wrinkled her nose. "Something smells funny." She covered her face with both hands. "Are you sure this is your daddy's house?"

"The smell is bleach." Cassie sniffed harder. "And garbage?"

Van nodded ever so slightly.

She stared at the faded paint and worn appliances. How had this looked before Van started cleaning? "Can I see Dad tonight? Does the hospital have late visiting hours?"

"What about—" He looked at Hope.

Cassie had known people would treat her and Hope like freaks, but she hadn't expected Van to be the first. "I'll manage. Thanks for your help." She went to the door, forcing him to follow, and then ushered him through. "And for looking after Dad."

On the porch, Van turned, opening his mouth, but Cassie had stopped worrying about manners. She shut the door.

And locked it. Tight as a drum.

THE MOON HUNG above thick trees. Van stared at it as he measured each step to his car.

His hand shook so much he could barely hit the button for entry. He stared at the house and wished he'd opened all the blinds. Whatever Cassie was doing, she wasn't letting in light or prying eyes.

Whatever she was doing… Finding something to feed her daughter. He got in the car and grabbed the steering wheel to keep from crashing his fists through his windshield.

His wife had given birth to that rapist's child.

His wife loved that animal's child. Love for Hope was a coat she wore—a second skin—a part of her he'd seen the moment the girl had called her name.

Damn her. Damn her to hell along with that bastard who'd stolen everything from him.

No.

That made it sound as if the rape had been her fault. He'd never thought that, never blamed her, never wanted her anywhere but at his side.

But it didn't feel as if five years had passed. He was still living that last night they'd tried to make love. His head swimming with images of that guy forcing her, he'd had to get away or punch the damn wall.

She hadn't understood. It was almost as if

she'd preferred thinking he couldn't stand being near her.

And tonight, she'd sprung Hope on him like another test. He'd failed again, but how could she expect the people who'd loved her to accept a constant, living reminder of the worst moments in their lives?

So, he hadn't thrown a party. He hadn't said anything to hurt Hope or Cassie, either. Why couldn't Cassie give him a break?

He looked up at the closed windows and the door whose locks still clanked and clicked in his ears. Five years, and it was as if she'd left last night and come home this morning.

All the feelings were so familiar. Fear, anger, dread.

And somewhere down deep, the love he hadn't been able to abandon or smother. No other woman had ever made him forget Cassie.

He'd been stranded in a time capsule since the evening she'd left him outside her lawyer's office. Him still swearing he'd make her love him again. Her looking sad. Out of his reach.

And early on, whenever he'd suggested he come to Washington to see her, she'd refused. Finally, she'd said her life would be easier and she'd forget the past better if she never again saw anyone connected with it.

Especially him.

He took a last look at the windows, like eyes closed against the world. Cassie had made enough rules for him and her father. Surely Leo was a living illustration that Cassie's way led to disaster.

Van made his own rules in every other part of his life. If Cassie wanted to throw away love, she'd have to say so, flat out.

He turned the key in the ignition and then pulled his cell from his pocket. Cassie took three rings to answer.

"Hello?"

If she'd sounded certain, instead of wary, maybe he'd have backed off. If she hadn't sounded afraid...

"Don't start dinner. I'll bring something back."

"I don't want you to come back."

"I don't blame you. I didn't treat Hope right and I'm sorry."

"She deserves better, and so do I."

Before, he'd have handled her with kid gloves. She'd been hurt, inside and out, and he couldn't hurt her more.

"Cassie." If he gave in, he'd lose any chance of finding out if they could still love each other. "I don't want to hurt that kid, but she reminds me of—" He couldn't say *her father.* If he did, he'd never look the child in the eye again. "She reminds me of what happened. Give me a chance to live with it."

"Are you crazy? I'm not coming back here.

You and I have been divorced for almost five years. We're over."

"Your father is extremely ill. You won't throw him into some nursing facility and run away."

"I will," she said through what sounded like gritted teeth.

"I know you."

"You're living in a crazy dream. You need treatment as much as my father."

"You might be right, but I've never said good-bye to you. I don't want to give up."

"On what? On nothing. It's been nothing since the night I left here."

"Do you think I'm proud of feeling this way? I'm a man. I don't want to run after a woman who couldn't be more clear about not wanting to be with me. But I think you were lying five years ago about not wanting us in your life, because you were afraid for your child. I have to know if we can still care for each other." He tapped his fist against the steering wheel. "Don't make me talk about feelings, Cassie. And don't make me beg."

Her silence stretched so long he pulled the phone away from his ear to see if the signal had faded or she'd hung up.

"Mommy," said a small voice on Cassie's side of the connection, "I'm really hungry."

"So I'll be back," Van said. "With dinner for both of you."

"For all of us?" Cassie asked.

He stiffened. "Are you inviting me or preparing yourself?"

She took a deep breath, but he was holding his. "Maybe a little of both."

"That's a start," he said. "I'll be back." He hung up before she could change her mind.

She might be right. What kind of man held on to a woman who'd turned her back on him in the most final of divorce decrees five years ago?

But she'd kept information to herself then. She'd been pregnant. With a rapist's child, but she'd been his wife and she'd been carrying a child. He'd loved her. He'd had a right to know— or to tell her he couldn't face it.

He wasn't sure he could face it now.

He pulled away from the curb, not letting thoughts of Hope reignite his old anger. She was a child, not someone to blame.

And he was through giving up on everything that had mattered because Cassie didn't believe in him. It was his turn to take charge.

For the first time in a long time, he felt a little hope.

He drove to the town's new overpriced luxury market, parking next door at the *Honesty Sentinel* because everyone who wanted to see and be seen had already taken all the open spots at Posh Victuals.

The second he hit the aromatic air inside, his stomach muttered with guttural hunger. He flattened his hand against his belly, but in the Babel of dinnertime shopping, no one else noticed.

He waited in line at the Poshly Prepared Pasta counter. A high school girl, wearing a checkered napkin folded artfully into a cap, finally got through the three customers before him.

"What may I feed you, sir?"

As if she were wearing a toga and offering grapes. "What do you have that will make a four-year-old girl happy?"

"Huh?" She glanced around the counters as if seeking help. No one materialized.

"I have a friend who's just arrived in town with her four-year-old daughter, and they haven't eaten. I'd like to take them some dinner."

Lowering her voice, she leaned toward him. "I'm supposed to talk you into buying the more expensive stuff, but take the spaghetti. Kids always like spaghetti. I have a little brother, and he can't get enough of the stuff we make here."

"Perfect. Pack it up."

"Just for the girl? Would you like a whole dinner? Or a child's spaghetti?"

"Dinner for three."

"Okeydoke."

"Do you have a meatless sauce?"

She nodded.

"I'd better take two orders of that." Cassie hadn't eaten meat for years before she'd left, and she might have persuaded her daughter to eat the same crazy way.

With deft hands, the girl packed a meal in takeout cartons. Pasta, a container of sauce, a larger one without meat, and garlic bread, so rich with spicy scents his stomach grumbled again. Louder.

The girl must have heard. Her mouth twitched, but she was too polite to mention it.

She added vegetable antipasto, a tossed salad and two containers of tiramisu. He stopped her in time to ask for crème brûlée for Cassie.

"Just warm everything up. If you boil the pasta for two minutes, it'll be better than new." She leaned in again. "I add olive oil to the water. Amazing."

"Thanks." He found her badge beneath a wavy ponytail. "Rita."

"My pleasure. Here's hoping your friends enjoy."

His friend had probably changed her mind about letting him in—and changed the locks.

Back at Leo's house, he parked in the driveway behind Cassie's rental and carried their dinner to the front door, tapping the newly painted porch with his fingertips to make sure it was dry. He rang the bell and then waved the bags in front of the wood to spread the delicious aromas. That market might have a froufrou name, but their cooking smelled great.

Nothing happened on the other side of the Warne door. He backed up and looked around one of the porch stanchions, but the blinds remained shut tight. If the lights were on, not one sliver of illumination leaked through.

He rang the bell again. Would she really change her mind? Could she lock him out of her life again?

The door opened, and Cassie stared at him, accusation and embarrassment on her face.

"How long did it take you to decide?" he asked, fighting a smile.

She stared at his mouth, and resentment firmed her beautiful lips. "I'm letting you in, but it doesn't mean anything." It should have sounded churlish, but her sad eyes made him feel responsible.

"Whatever makes you feel all right, Cassie. Where's—" he cursed himself for the three seconds it took to say her name "—Hope?"

"That's why I don't want you around. I don't doubt you mean well and, obviously, I'm some sort of penance to you." She lowered her voice. "But every time you look at my little girl, you'll see that man." She said it without a shudder, as if that didn't happen to her. "Or you'll wonder why I kept her." She took both bags.

He caught the door in one hand, half expecting her to close it, and then he took back the heavier bag. "I'd never hurt you—or Hope."

This time her daughter's name stopped her for a second. "Not on purpose." She nudged him with the other bag. Cassie, who'd never had a violent bone in her body, actually tried to push him outside. "But you can't help—and your feelings hurt me more than anything *he* ever did."

It was a kick in the gut. He swallowed—twice—before he was able to speak. "Don't ever say that again." The connection between his mouth and brain seemed to break. Finally, he managed to pry his tongue off the roof of his mouth. "Don't compare me to him."

He turned for the door, but she caught him.

"I'm sorry," she said, and he believed her because her eyes shone with unshed tears and her mouth trembled. "It just came out. I didn't mean—"

"Let it go. There are some things you and I can't talk about." Nor could he explain he'd been walking through life blind, not living since she'd left him. "I was surprised about Hope. A man doesn't expect his former—" He glanced toward the kitchen. "I never thought about you having a baby and me not knowing, but none of this is her fault. I want her to feel comfortable around me, and you'd better want that, too, because someone has to look after her while you visit your father."

Maybe Hope could hang out with one of the nurses for the few minutes it would take for him to— "I'm the closest thing to family he's had for the past few days. You need me to remind him who you are."

Van's speech, half apology and a whole lot of assumption, hung in the air.

Cassie stared, her mouth half-open until she noticed she was catching flies and closed it. "Remind him?" The bag slipped in her arms. She managed to catch it. "You honestly think he won't know me?"

Van eyed her right back as if he was worried she might also be losing her memory. "I told you that, Cassie."

"I didn't understand." She turned with the bag, not certain where to go next. "How am I going to make sure no one tells him about—I don't care if he hates me, but I don't want him to hurt her." Van's reaction to Hope had proved she was right to shield her daughter from everyone in Honesty. "Plus, I don't want him to get worse. Making him angry could easily make him sicker."

"What are you talking about? You think he hates you?"

She lifted her head, an animal scenting a challenge. "I liked you better when you couldn't hide anything you felt." Including the fact that he'd blamed her, too. "He thought what happened was my fault."

"He was scared. Still is, but he doesn't hate you."

Trust Van to protect her father. She went toe to toe with the only man she'd ever loved more than her dad. "I could never blame Hope for something like that. That's how I know his love wasn't enough, and he does blame me."

Deep down, she realized she was still accusing Van, too. She couldn't help it. His rejection—turning from her in their bed, stepping away from her as they'd gazed together out of their kitchen window—those moments lived under her skin, thorns too sharp to bear.

They'd argued until he had no more words, and hers only made him angry.

"Your father isn't well."

"He was fine five years ago." A new rush of resentment shocked her. She had to get a grip. "I'm sorry." She rubbed her forehead. "Seeing you and being here brings it all back."

"I didn't like your answers to our problems then. I still don't." Answers. Nice, antiseptic way to describe ripping out her own heart and throwing it onto a barbed-wire fence.

"You don't get a choice," she said, not to be unkind but to make him see it was too late to change things.

Faltering, Van turned to a safer subject. "Leo's

worse when he's tired, and what about Hope? I'll be glad to look after her, but she'll have to go with us when I introduce you to him."

"I can explain if he doesn't know me." She hated the thought of accepting his help. As if coming back had turned her into the naive young woman who'd married her personal Prince Charming, the habit of leaning on Van tempted her. "And Hope doesn't know you. I'm not comfortable leaving her with anyone."

"Like it or not, I'm not just anyone."

"Close enough."

He looked her straight in the eye and pretended not to have heard. "I could ask my sister to come to the hospital."

"Beth." Her heart ached. She'd lost more than her father and Van. "I've missed her."

"You could have stayed in touch."

"How would I have asked her not to tell you about Hope?"

"You couldn't." He lifted the other bag of food. "Dinner's getting cold."

Hope appeared in the kitchen doorway. "Mommy, I'm starwing. I need foods."

"Coming, sweetie." Cassie led the way. "I'll call the hospital and see if my father's still awake."

In the kitchen, Hope climbed back into a chair. The water Cassie had set to boil in a saucepan on the stove was still, the gas beneath it turned off.

Hope looked up as Cassie put two and two together. "I did it."

The stove was like theirs at home, far from here. Her little girl wanted to be a big girl as quick as she could and never thought about saucepan handles. "I've asked you not to mess with stoves when I'm not in the room."

"I'm okay. It's like ours. I knew how."

"Hope, I've asked you…"

"I'm sorry, Mommy."

"Do you like to help cook, Hope?" Van started removing paper cartons from his sack. The poisonous resentment in his voice had faded.

He was so very friendly.

"We were gonna have those instant grits." She pointed at the counter.

He made a face at the box. "I've saved you from an ugly fate."

"Mommy likes 'em." She slid out of her chair and went to his elbow.

"You're not such a big fan?"

He still hadn't looked into her innocent face.

"I don't mind 'em." Lying, Hope smiled at Cassie, offering her loyalty.

"Maybe you'll like this stuff instead." Setting the last carton on the table, he looked at Hope and a smile spread across his face. A real smile. Wide, warm. Real.

Hope laughed out loud. "I was kinda scared to

come here, but you're nice, Mr. Van. I like your face."

He laughed, too. Slowly, his hand curved around the back of Hope's head.

For a split second, before he pulled back and whisked the bag off the table.

CHAPTER FOUR

VAN FOLDED the Posh bag as deliberately as any bit of paper anywhere had ever been folded, and then he stared at the recycling bin, stunned by Cassie's look of relief.

She must love her daughter more than he'd imagined if she thought he could forget the past so easily.

"Mr. Van, are you saving that bag?"

He pushed it into the bin and got himself under control. Ridiculous that a little girl could do this to him. But it was what she stood for—those hellish images he had never escaped.

"No." He choked as his throat tightened. "I'm not saving it."

He turned. Cassie was waiting, still watchful.

"What *did* you bring?" Cassie asked with a hand toward the cartons.

"Antipasto, spaghetti, tiramisu for Hope and me and crème brûlée for you."

"I smell the spaghetts." Hope's nose quivered like a kitten's. "And look at the salad, Mommy."

She prodded the one see-through package. "Can I have your cootons?"

"Croutons." Her voice was absent. "Spaghetts are Hope's favorites."

There was more in her tone. An extra warning. She looked at her daughter with her heart literally in her eyes and more love than Van suspected she'd ever felt for him. Hope owned that much of her. Cassie would fight with her last breath to keep her little girl safe.

Even from him. As if he'd hurt a baby.

She took down plates and salad dishes from the cabinet. Then she helped Hope open the plastic container. "What else did you want to talk about?" Her briskness suggested he make it fast and beat it.

"I didn't come back just to talk about your father."

She found serving utensils and scooped salad onto Hope's dish without looking up. "He's all that's left. Face it, Van."

"No." With Hope hanging on every nuance, he couldn't elaborate.

Cassie just looked at him. Then she popped the tops off the other cartons and started to add food to her daughter's plate.

"Wait." Van reached for her hand, but she backed up. Message taken. "I need to warm up the pasta."

Cassie shrugged. "Okay. I'd better call the hospital, but you can start now with your salad, baby."

"Goodie."

"Will you talk to Mr. Van while I'm gone?"

"Su-u-re." Hope grinned over her mother's hand pouring dressing on her salad.

"I'll use the phone in Dad's study."

Like that, she was gone. He hardly knew how to talk to any children, other than his nephew, who was about eight years older than Hope and didn't remind him of the worst days of his life.

"Have you ever flown before?" He grabbed a topic out of thin air.

She shook her head. Her hair slipped into her salad. He had to brush it over her shoulder.

"It made my ears feel funny," she said.

"Mine always do, too." He moved to the stove and turned on the gas beneath the saucepan to heat up the water again. "Does your mom let you chew gum?"

"I love gum, Mr. Van. You got some?"

"I sure do, and I'd be happy to share if your mother doesn't mind. It helps when you fly."

"Why?"

Wouldn't you know? "I guess it opens up some tube in your ears." He shook the pan to hurry the water along. Unnerved by a small girl. "Something like that—I think."

"My mommy told me to yawn, but I couldn't always. I drooled once."

She startled him into laughing. "I've done that, too. Try gum next time."

"When we go back. I'm in school, you know."

"Kindergarten?"

She snorted and stuffed a forkful of salad into her mouth. "How old do you think I am?" she asked around the greens. "I'm not a big kid yet."

"Pretty big," he said. She was tall for her age, but she looked kind of thin to him. Thank God the water started to bubble. He turned the pasta into the saucepan. "This stuff will be done in a second."

She poked a finger into the sauce. "This is cold, too."

He glanced toward the doorway, suspecting Cassie might not be big on poking food or talking around salads. "I'll warm it up," he said as he picked up the container and dumped its contents into a bowl, which he put in the microwave.

"Don't tell Mommy I touched it. She makes me wash my hands all the time."

"Mothers can be like that."

"Like what?"

Cassie had walked in silently.

"Kind of picky," he said, without thinking. Hope giggled and then covered her mouth.

He grinned. Maybe feelings could start to

change. She was a funny little girl, and he wasn't quite nuts enough to think she'd be her so-called father reincarnated.

"How's Leo?"

"Asleep. They said he's restless at night, so I should leave him alone until morning. Will you tell me exactly what's happening with him?"

He'd tell her anything she asked for in the soft voice that reminded him of the way it had been before.

But before he could answer, she touched Hope's hair. "Later," she said.

Silence stretched between them, while Van remembered how to breathe.

Hope filled up the quiet. "I took a shower." She plucked at her pink Dora the Explorer pajamas. "The shower smelled funny." Hope sniffed. "But so does this kitchen. My house smells like—what is it, Mommy?" She peered up at Cassie, who was scooping pasta onto Hope's plate. "We like cimmanon candles."

"We use bleach sometimes, too." Cassie's quick glance told Van she could imagine how the house had looked before. As she took her seat, Van was glad she hadn't seen the filth her father had been abiding in. He moved around Cassie to ladle sauce over Hope's pasta. Cassie sprinkled parmesan on top. "Now, eat up, Hope. It's way past your bedtime."

"Will I see my grampa tomorrow?"

"I'm not sure." Another quick look included Van. He had a feeling Leo wouldn't be ready for Hope for a while.

But then again, he was assuming Cassie would stay until her father was well. Maybe, considering her fears for Hope, he was being too optimistic.

Maybe he was trying to re-create a past with a woman who no longer existed. He missed a life that she'd forgotten.

BEFORE SHE FINISHED her dessert, Hope began nodding. Cassie pulled the tiramisu away from her just in time to keep her face out of the plate.

"Take her up," Van said. "I'll clean this up and put the leftovers in the fridge."

Cassie wanted to turn him down and send him away. She hated needing his help. He might be looking for their old relationship, but those feelings were either gone or behind an impenetrable wall for her. That life might have happened to some other woman. It was as if she'd heard about their marriage in intimate detail but hadn't actually lived it.

"You don't have to tidy up," she said. "Just take your coffee into the living room." It was spick-and-span, though the dining room door remained closed. "I'll be down and we can talk."

He nodded, but the sounds of dishwashing followed her up the stairs.

She helped Hope brush her teeth and then she tucked her daughter into bed. Staring at her baby's silky, dark hair splayed across one of her mother's best guest pillowcases, she tried to believe they were back in her old house. Impossible.

On her way out, she pulled the door almost closed. At the bottom of the stairs, Van waited, a mug of coffee for himself and one for her as well.

She took it and sipped. Someone else might have lived those days with Van, but he knew her, including her preference for one sugar and plenty of cream.

"Time stands still in Honesty," she said.

"I noticed the days going by."

Uncomfortable with what those words implied, she moved to the couch and sat down. Landing on a lump, she lifted the cushion to find an assortment of bundled socks. "They all look clean."

"There's been no rhyme or reason."

His tone reflected her horror.

"It's so confusing, why he's done these things. I looked up Alzheimer's after we talked last night. Compulsive behaviors make patients feel more secure, but the behavior often makes no sense." She lifted a sock. "This is not my father."

"Lang Baxter's his doctor. He tells me all of this could be a result of the other things he's suffering from—malnutrition, depression, possibly dementia—but it doesn't have to be Alzheimer's."

"What it's called doesn't matter." She searched his face for a hint of her ex-husband. She'd known how to talk to him before the rape, but had she loved Van too much to be his friend now? "You obviously still care for my father."

"How do you feel about him?"

"I'm not sure." Honesty came easier with Hope safely in bed. "I needed him so much after what happened." She set her coffee on the table beside the couch's elegant carved arm. "But I came home. That must mean something." She scooped out the socks, leaving them beside her to discourage Van from sharing the couch, and then cradled her coffee. "I had to deal with the rape," she said, "so I could learn to love Hope, but I still needed my father."

"But not me," Van said.

"I'm not looking back on you as the love I long for. We're over."

He took the armchair across from her. "I thought I'd dealt with losing you until I saw your father on that bridge."

"Why did that change anything about us?"

"Leo and you and I were family. We all gave up too easily and now I know why you really left."

"Your family is Beth and Eli. Hope and I are a

family, and I'll find a way to include my father, but Van, it's too late for you and me."

Pain widened the green eyes she'd loved so much. For a second, she felt like water swirling toward a drain, but she took control. Caring for him was an old habit masquerading as actual feelings.

"Van, don't force me to be unkind. I haven't been dreaming of coming back to you."

"I haven't dreamed of that, either, but I've never understood why you had to leave me, and I haven't managed to let you go."

"You don't have a choice." Even if she'd consider returning, how could he ever come to terms with the truth about Hope? "Tell me about Dad. Please," she said, her voice thick enough to betray her. She shouldn't have to beg him to stay away from the past as if he were the bad man who scared her.

"Okay. We'll get back to your father." He barely looked at her, turning away. "He doesn't always live in the here and now. Sometimes your mother is alive. Sometimes I don't exist."

"What does he say about me?"

"He doesn't say much. I'm not sure how he'll act when he sees you, Cass."

That nickname again. To Van, it was obviously just something to call her.

"He knows you've been estranged," he continued.

"Because of the way he treated me back then. I couldn't risk—" She massaged her temple. "I have to stop being defensive." She lifted her head. "Are you trying to tell me he won't be able to live alone?"

"I'm not a doctor," Van said, "but I saw him this afternoon. He was cleaner, but not better. He thought the hospital staff would try to steal his keys and rob the place." He nodded toward the ceiling, signifying the house. "I can't see him taking care of himself."

Cassie froze, head to toe. Her dad. Pride had been his favorite coat.

"He can't help it," Van said.

"I know. He was a good father once, and maybe the rape did something to him, too. Either way, it's not that I don't want to take care of him. I just can't face Hope taking grief from the people here. I'll have to take him back to Washington."

"He won't want to go. Think how he'll feel. Nothing and no one will be familiar."

"Meaning me?" She shook her head. "Never mind. I know what you mean, but I have to think of Hope first. She's the child."

"And she could be happy here, too. Give us a chance." He set down his cup. "People might be curious, but no one would be aggressive. When I came over here to check on the house, Trey Lockwood was working on the porch. Honesty is your home, and the people here care about you."

"It *was* my home."

"What do you do in Washington, Cass? I know nothing about your life since you left."

"I own a women's shelter with two friends."

"Own?" He looked surprised. "I thought they were nonprofit."

"It can be done. We're less liable to state interference, and we feel we can do more for the women who need us."

"It doesn't bother you to see them in trouble like you were?"

"Sure, but I want to help them. Making sure they're safe makes me feel—" She couldn't say *safer* to Van. She didn't want him to know she was afraid. Ever. "Anyway, I've moved on since I left here. And I can't just walk away from the life I've made in Washington."

Van reached for his cup, and when it toppled, they both tried to grab it. Cassie caught it, along with a handful of tepid coffee.

"I'm sorry. Are you burned?"

"It's not hot anymore."

Van hurried to the kitchen and returned with a cloth to clean up the spill. Cassie passed him in the hall, taking both their cups back.

They said nothing as they walked by each other, but she sensed him, a force like the pull of gravity. She leaned on the kitchen counter, resisting the laws of nature.

"You all right?"

His voice, tight with concern, dragged her around. He was tall, silent, a little leaner, a hint of silver among the dark blond strands of his hair.

She fought her need for him. She prayed the long-lost habit of wanting him more than her own next breath wouldn't consume her.

Cassie had practiced a natural-looking cheerful smile until she could no longer say when it was real and when it was a performance. She put it on for him. "Would you mind asking Beth if she'd look after Hope tomorrow while I see Dad?"

He nodded. "Visiting hours start at eight in the morning. When should I pick you up?"

A cold chill made her vulnerable. "Eight is good."

Van left without another word, but his pain lingered in the hall. Cassie pretended not to notice.

A YEAR AGO, Van had been his sister's refuge. After her lodge had burned, he'd given her and her son a home while they'd rebuilt. He'd also introduced her to the man who'd become her husband, his other unexpected guest at the time, Aidan Nikolas.

Aidan had moved the offices of Nikolas Enterprises to a small cabin down the hill from Beth's fishing lodge, and they'd married just after the New Year. Now, deep in the next winter, Van was less than pleased to find himself driving down Beth's gravel lane to beg for advice from his baby sister. He'd always been the one who took care of her.

He knocked on the door, but there was no answer. He knocked again. Then he flipped his phone open and called her cell.

"Hey, Van. What's up?"

"Where are you?"

"Watching Eli's hockey practice. Where are you?"

"At your place. When are you coming home?"

"Do you need me? I'll come now." She paused a moment. "No, wait. If Aidan and Eli are around, we won't get a minute to ourselves. I'll send them home after practice and you can meet me for coffee at the ice rink."

"I'll drive you home afterward."

"Otherwise, I'd have to walk," she pointed out. "See you at the rink."

"Okay." He was pathetically grateful. He'd never admitted how he still felt about Cassie, but Beth had always known. Far from empathizing, she'd suggested he get on with life instead of burying himself in the past.

Unfortunately, he'd never realized how smart his sister was.

A few minutes later, he parked in front of the ice rink. Across the glowing white surface, he watched Aidan and Beth and Eli saying goodbye beside the family SUV.

Aidan pulled her close. She patted Eli's arm. He twisted away, and then Aidan, laughing, slid his hand across her belly.

Van observed, poleaxed. Eli made a gag-himself gesture and jumped into the SUV's front seat. Beth and Aidan hugged each other a last time.

Van felt an outsider looking in on a real family. Lifting his face to the star-pinned sky, he searched for solace in the cold December night, in the smoke from every chimney along the town square, in the familiar evergreen scent of his life in the Virginia forest.

He could have taken his business anywhere. He could have made a life apart from the memories that had frozen him in time.

He walked around the fence that separated the ice from the playground. Beth met him near the concession stand.

She hugged him. "I'm starving. I think I'll have a hot dog with my cocoa."

"You don't want to skate?"

Her eyes lit up, but then she twisted her mouth and grazed her stomach with her hand, betraying herself.

"You're pregnant, Beth?"

Her eyebrows went up. "What are you, psychic?"

"Nosy. I saw you from over there." He pointed to his car.

She grinned, her pride touching. "Don't say anything yet, okay?"

He caught some of her happiness. "Who would I tell?"

"Small towns." She lifted both hands to include their whole small-town world. But then she turned to him, grinning as wide as she could. "It's so early we haven't told anyone. Mostly, the only difference I feel is twenty-four-hour morning sickness."

He held her close. "This time will be different," he told her. She'd gotten pregnant with Eli in high school and had made a bad marriage. "This time, you're with someone who loves you. I'm happy for you, little sis."

"You look happy. A second ago, you didn't." She took his sleeve and led him in a beeline toward the concession stand. "You can treat me while I find a table, and after you bring me sustenance you can tell me what's upsetting you."

He took orders from her for the first time in his life. But there she was, all Mother Earth and I-have-a-plan, and he didn't know what to do next.

He ordered hot dogs and cocoa, tempted because he hadn't been able to choke down much of his meal with Cassie and Hope. He took the food back to the table Beth had snagged. "Should you be eating this?"

"Talk slow, and I'll eat yours, too." She unwrapped the mustard-smeared waxed paper and took a bite, sighing immediately with contentment.

"Cassie's home."

She sat up straight. "Good." The hot dog went gently to the table. "Her father needs her."

That simple, as if Cassie were anyone, not the woman she'd claimed as a sister and the best friend whose loss she'd mourned like a death.

"Didn't you expect she'd come?" he asked.

"You're looking for a fight." She returned to savaging her hot dog. "I didn't assume either way, so back off, brother. She left here plenty mad at both you and Leo. We all lost her because of her father."

"And me?"

"I never understood the way she was with you after the—afterward. I always thought I'd have turned to the man I loved, but neither of us was in her shoes, so we can't know what she was thinking."

"Maybe she should have given me a hint or two."

Beth looked up, startled, as she pried the top off her cocoa. "I've never heard you say one word against Cassie."

"How do you blame a woman who's been through that?" He shoved his wrapped hot dog across the table. "I don't blame her now, but I don't know how my marriage ended."

"I was never sure it did end for you."

"Cassie doesn't want to hear that, either."

"You told her?" Beth sipped cocoa, her eyes like half-dollars above the cup's white paper rim.

A shout and sparks rose from the bonfire at the other end of the rink. They both stopped to inspect the knot of teenagers partying.

"Last year, I would have assumed Eli was over there, looking for trouble," Beth remarked.

"But this year, he's a happy kid with a good father figure and a little sibling on the way."

"Let's hope he didn't count on remaining an only child."

He squeezed her hand. "Eli will love the baby, and besides, he has Dr. Maria to smooth over the rough edges."

"Maybe you should talk to Maria Keaton. She looks like she's sixteen, but she's an able therapist. I'm not sure it's healthy to still want a broken marriage five years after your wife walked away."

"Don't hurt yourself trying to pull punches, Beth."

"Face it. You should have moved on and found someone else."

"Okay, so I didn't want your advice after all, but I do have a favor to ask."

With a motherly pat on his shoulder, she leaned into the light.

"You have a whipped-cream mustache," he said.

"Hunger is making you cranky. You should have eaten this hot dog yourself," Beth said as she picked it up. "I already put together a tomato and cucumber salad. I left a roast in the Dutch oven, and I'm going to open some canned green beans from the garden. You could join us for dinner."

"A third meal? I've wasted enough food already, and I can't believe you plan to eat again after two of those." She took another bite of her "snack."

"I may not finish yours." She chewed with closed eyes. "I need the facts. You're surprised to feel the way you always have for Cassie?"

"You feel nothing for Campbell?" Her deadbeat first husband had been no one to pine for.

She shuddered. "But if I lost Aidan, I don't picture turning everything off. You didn't choose the divorce. You just didn't fight it. Why?"

"I think she wanted me to prove nothing had changed between us." He drank some cocoa and burned his tongue. As he waved a hand in front of his mouth, Beth grinned. "Everything changed except that I loved her. I was her husband. I was supposed to protect her. I know, Beth. Don't lunge across the table—I'm a cliché and a caveman, but I loved my wife, and when I looked at her, I saw what that man did to her…."

Beth took his hand again. "This is why you need Dr. Maria."

"I'm serious." He'd been right to hide how much he still cared. If even his sister thought he needed therapy, maybe he did have a problem.

"Forget what happened then. Do what you have to now. And for pity's sake, if you still love Cassie, tell her. Fight for her."

"She has a baby—a little girl—she's four." He took another sip. Boiling liquid sawdust.

Beth stared at him, slowly comprehending. Tears floated in her eyes. "She took a baby away from you? I don't believe it. Not Cassie."

He shook his head and didn't bother to hide his own horror. Beth grabbed her stomach.

"You're sure she's the right age?" Beth asked.

"Cassie told me. Hope is his. She didn't believe she could stay here and raise the child."

"I could kill him."

"I should have."

"How hard is it to get into a prison?"

Wind whistled between them, spiked with the laughter of the skaters. They stared at each other, both startled at the intensity of their hatred. But his was partly for himself as well.

"Hope is her name?" Beth shoved the rest of her food and drink away. "What's she like?"

"Sweet. A kid." She was more than that—trusting, gentle, happy to meet him, never knowing what he'd seen when he'd first seen her.

"What would any woman do in Cassie's place?" Beth asked.

"I don't give a damn about any woman." Too hurt for too long, he had no room to be compassionate. "I want my old life, with my wife and my home and my family. By now we'd have had children of our own. Leo wouldn't be stuck in a hospital bed in a world that never existed. Cassie would be safe and happy and loved." He raked his hands over his face. "I can't stand thinking."

After a moment, Beth pulled his hands down to the table. "Is Cassie with her dad tonight?"

"No. I'm supposed to take her in the morning. I'm afraid he won't recognize her so I wouldn't let her go alone."

"Let her? She stood for that?"

"Don't sound all speculative. It doesn't mean anything. I came to ask if you'd look after Hope while we visit Leo."

"Did you tell her you were asking me?"

"She thought it was a good idea, too."

"No mother would want her baby to meet a grandfather in the shape Leo's in."

"The thing is, you can't—I mean, it's not Hope's fault that she's—"

Beth looked confused.

"She doesn't know the truth about herself."

Beth sat back, grabbing the sides of her bench. "I'm no monster. I'd never hurt a child's feelings."

It was so easy for her? "I think I may be one."

Again, he heard the crackle of fire, the scraping of skates and childish laughter that seemed unnatural and harsh. "She's a good kid, and funny. I found myself laughing at her—with her. But I still see him. It's why I lost Cassie in the first place. Every time I tried to touch her, I saw him, and she thought I didn't want her."

"Didn't you tell her the truth?"

He nodded, or he might have shaken his head. He couldn't tell which. "She never believed me."

"Whatever happens now, you have a second chance to salvage something with Cassie, even if it's only friendship. You just have to be a decent man. She knows how difficult this is for you. She had to face the truth about Hope's conception, too."

"I'm not allowed to equivocate. Cassie wants me to care for Hope without a second thought." He stood. "Sorry. I didn't actually plan to tell you all this. Can I pick you up at seven in the morning?"

"Are we leaving now?"

"I have to—yes."

She came around the table to hug him tight. "You can't help being a good man. I believe in you."

"I'm not sure it's enough."

She patted his cheek, apparently overwhelmed by motherly impulses. "I'd bet it is."

"She's not even planning to stay here. I don't know what kind of future—"

"Maybe you'll have to go with her. She must have a job, and her daughter will have made friends. You can do your work anywhere."

"Beth, she runs a shelter in Washington. After what she went through, she counsels other women who've also been raped. I hate the thought of her reliving that every day."

"She was always going to do social work of some kind. Maybe treating other women helps her heal."

"That's pretty much what she said." He hugged his sister, grateful for her common sense even if he couldn't share her faith. "Let's go, Beth. Is it okay if I pick you up at seven tomorrow?"

CHAPTER FIVE

"MOMMY." Hope's voice, punctuated by a bounce that nearly tossed Cassie out of her bed. "Mommy, time to get up. I'm starwing again."

"Okay." Cassie tried to pry one sleepy eye open. "What are the numbers on the clock?"

Bounce. "A six." Bounce. "A three." Bounce, bounce. Cassie's brains began to scramble. "And a circle."

"A circle?" She pushed herself onto one elbow, searching for the digital display. "Six-thirty. We'd better get moving, punkin'. Mr. Van will be here before we know it."

"More food."

Cassie caught Hope's arm. "You're going to fall down and break your crown."

With her sleeper-clad feet pointed as professionally as any ballerina's, Hope collapsed backward in giggles. Cassie must be funnier than she knew.

Morning people. She rolled over to tickle Hope. "Are you really hungry? Oatmeal? Grits? Gruel?"

"What's gru, Mommy?"

Cassie sat up, pulling her little girl into her lap. "I don't actually know. You want some toast as an appetizer while I take a shower?"

"I watch Dora?"

"You wouldn't take advantage of a mom for some TV time, would you?"

Giggling with a four-year-old's joy, she nodded. "And choplit milk?"

"Yup, but only 'cause we're in a special place, and you've never been here before."

"When we go home, I have to eat normal and no TV?"

"Right."

But when would they go home? She helped Hope into her robe and steered her down the stairs to the kitchen. They made toast together, smearing it with strawberry jam, and then they took the plate back upstairs.

Feeling just a smidge guilty, Cassie settled Hope in front of the TV with her toast. Then she sped through a shower, dressed and whipped up an egg-and-cheese omelet. Hope was digging in when a knock came at the front door.

"I get it." Still chewing her first bite, Hope bolted, with Cassie hot on her heels. Hope yanked at the doorknob, but Cassie had to work the locks first.

Seeing Van set her heart pounding, but she didn't have to like it.

Then she saw Beth. She stepped into the wood-smoke-scented morning and threw her arms around the woman who'd been more sister than sister-in-law. She'd longed for Beth so many times in the past five years.

"Hi," she said, acknowledging Van's anxious glance over his sister's shoulder. She moved her daughter in front of her and laughed as her little girl immediately offered a hand to shake. "Hope, this is Beth."

Smiling with apparently unadulterated happiness, Beth squatted to meet Hope on her own level. "You look so much like your mommy. You know, she was my best friend when I was a little girl."

"My best friend is Susie Banner."

"Does Susie live in Washington?"

Hope nodded, and her hair fell around her shoulders. Cassie looked at Van, sharing her relief—her sheer joy—in Beth's welcome for her child.

"She gives me hope," Cassie said. Van's grin was affectionate, proud of his sister.

"I can see why." Beth straightened.

"I meant you," Cassie said.

"Oh." She looked startled. "I'd be proud to have such a little girl. My brother's been telling me about you, Hope."

"Who's your brother?"

"Mr. Van," Cassie said. "And Beth has a son named Eli."

"Can I play with him?" Hope asked.

"He's a big boy so he's at school, but he might drop by after, if I'm still here," Beth said. "Do you mind if you and I hang out today?"

"I dunno." Hope scuffed the lined foot of her sleeper. "Are you a nice lady, Miss Beth?"

Again, Cassie glanced at Van as Beth laughed, totally engrossed in Hope. He was smiling, his eyes softer on her little girl.

"The nicest," Beth said. "Do you have favorite books? I love to read, and later we could take a walk."

"Walk," Hope said. "Walk, Mom?"

Her first thought was no. Someone might see Hope and get curious enough to ask a neighborly but blunt question of Beth.

Who knew how long they'd have to stay in Honesty? She couldn't sequester a four-year-old child inside the prison walls of a house in the name of protecting her.

"A walk is a great idea. Thanks, Beth—" But Hope had already started hauling her new friend upstairs for a sweater.

"Hope, you have to finish your breakfast."

"Don't worry. I'll sort it out," Beth said. "Take your time. We'll be fine, and Van knows my cell number if you need to call."

Cassie ran to the bottom of the stairs. "Hope, I need to talk to you."

"Don't worry." Beth read her mind. "If anyone asks questions, I'll put them off. I'm good at that."

"She is," Van said behind Cassie as Beth and Hope disappeared. "No interrogation too tough for her."

Cassie dropped her hands onto the banister. Without the others, the foyer felt too small. "Thanks for asking her to look after Hope."

"She was glad to."

"I owe you a lot."

"You owe me nothing."

She turned at last to face him. His face was rigid, but he dragged his hand across his mouth, and the lines around it eased.

"I care about you," he said. "It doesn't have to be a bad thing. I'm not even sure what it means."

"I can't think about going back to the way we were. I'm just relieved because I've been afraid to come home, and it's not as bad as I expected."

"The rape happened a long time ago, and no one ever blamed you."

"Let's not start this again."

"Once more," he said. "So you know where I stand. I think I've been in shock, trying to do what you wanted all these years." He stuck out his chin—at just the right angle for punching if she felt like it. "I was married to you, and I didn't want the divorce. I lost you because I couldn't stop seeing that animal hurting you."

"And now you see that when you look at Hope." He shook his head, but Cassie knew better. "Did you tell Beth the truth about her?"

"I had to when she thought Hope was mine and you kept her away from me."

"I understand you don't want people thinking she's yours, but that's not the worst thing they could think about me. No one will look at her with anything except sympathy if they think you're her father."

"You think they'd look at her differently if they knew the truth?"

"Don't sound so incredulous." She opened the closet door and yanked out her coat. "My own OB thought I must have lost my mind."

"People are going to ask."

"And if they do, I plan to make sure they know Hope is none of their business."

She tried to get her arms into her sleeves, but they refused to go. When Van reached out to assist, she jerked away. She couldn't stop herself. She started down the porch stairs as if she hadn't seen his helping hands.

"Cassie, I didn't mean to upset you. This is going to be difficult enough."

"I'm all right."

He said nothing, holding the car door for her.

He'd always done that, as if he hadn't noticed hardly any other guy still did those things.

He drove in silence. She was grateful. Anxiety crowded the breath in her lungs as they got closer to the hospital.

She stole a peek at Van as he parked. "Maybe I picked that argument," she said. "I'm scared about my dad."

"I don't blame you," he said. "But it doesn't change what I said."

The nurses watched them as they passed. It was such a small hospital there was hardly ever a rush, even in the E.R. Cassie recognized several of her high school classmates. Her chemistry lab partner, in a white coat, looked at her twice as he stepped onto the elevator when they got off on her father's floor.

"Cassie?" the guy said, surprised as the door began to close.

She smiled at him, but her mouth felt numb, and she was glad the doors shut before she had to speak. "Van, let's go straight to Dad's room. I don't think I can talk to anyone."

Nodding, he led the way, turning at a door on the right. He stood back for her, and she looked up, selfishly searching his eyes for comfort as she walked inside.

With unnecessary kindness, Van took her hand. She didn't want to find strength in his fingers twined with hers, but she squeezed back. At the last minute, she thought she might have been wrong to abandon her father.

Beyond a bathroom that jutted out into the rest of the room, she saw a small man, lying limp beneath ultrawhite sheets. Without Van, she might not have known him. He was ghostly, peering out of hollow, dark eyes. The bed swallowed him whole.

"You never told me…" She turned to Van. Was her father about to die?

"Mama," Leo said.

Horror washed over her, but her father's voice, rich with terror, seemed to belong to the child out of whose frightened eyes he stared.

Cassie made herself breathe. She half turned toward Van, her legs threatening to give.

"Mom?" Her father sounded less sure.

Gathering everything left of her fleeing strength, she stood on her own two feet and faced the truth about her father.

This was not going to be a fly-by-get-every-thing-organized trip.

He'd either have to come back to Washington with her and Hope, or they'd have to stay in Honesty with him.

She made it to the side of his bed and took his hand between both of hers. "It's me, Dad. I'm your daughter, Cassie."

His eyes slowly closed and then opened again as he scoured his faulty memory. "No," he said. "You won't come home. You hate me."

"I never hated you." She'd only craved the medicine of his unconditional love to heal the wounds that monster had opened in her soul.

Images fluttered through her mind, snapshots of a childhood she seemed to have borrowed. She saw her father kissing a Scooby-Doo Band-Aid on her elbow. She saw him climbing the knobby oak tree beside her window to coax her orange tabby back to the ground, while she and her mother, hand in hand, tried to talk them both down to safety.

Suited up like Andrew Carnegie, he'd talked to her third-grade class about being a bank teller when he'd been the bank's president, because Cassie had said his job was boring. He'd waited up for her the first nights she'd gone out with Van, despite the fact he'd loved her date as if he were a son.

Love refused to be predictable or reasonable.

Staying to help him because he was ill meant people would ask about Hope, but what else could she do? She couldn't even invite him to Washington until his health improved.

She hooked a chair with her foot and pulled it to his bedside so she didn't have to let go of his hand.

She settled next to him on one curled foot. "I love you, Dad. Tell me what's the matter and maybe you'll feel better."

VAN LEANED into a corner beside the door. His throat closed as Leo struggled to articulate what was wrong but finally contented himself with clutching Cassie's hand.

As the silence grew painful, she fixed a smile on her face and talked about herself. She talked about the Kind Heart, her shelter. She described her town house, the landscaping in her meager yard, her wish to buy a real house. At that, Leo became anxious and she backed off.

She never mentioned Hope.

"Do you remember him?" Leo pointed at Van.

She nodded. "I'll never forget, Dad. You won't either, will you?"

"I've been mean to him. I walked the other way when I saw him coming. I pretended I didn't know where you were, that I hadn't hired someone to find you."

Cassie's eyebrows went up. Leo's confession startled Van, too, but he was mainly grateful that the other man had remembered anything at all.

Maybe with Cassie holding his hand, Leo stood a chance.

"I thought you were my mom when I first saw you." His uncertain gaze roamed her face again.

"But you're my daughter." He half shook his head. "Aren't you?"

"Mmm-hmm." Her low-key answer made his question sound reasonable, even though her throat vibrated with the sound.

"Can I get you anything, Cassie?" Van felt the need to do something.

She stood. "Actually, I'm going to get some water. Dad, can I bring you some?"

Leo used both his shaking hands to rub his throat. "I'd like that. Thanks, honey. You'll come back?"

"Sure." Smiling, she took his large water cup and pushed through the door.

Van followed, wanting to pull her close. She was still Cassie. He still needed to make life right for her, a job he'd failed at.

"You don't have to stay, Van."

"You sound angry." He'd be pissed as hell with fate, too.

"No."

"It's all right, Cassie. Anyone would be upset."

"Nothing's all right."

Several heads turned their way. She lowered her voice. "I want to help him. Even I can see the past doesn't matter now." She straightened her shoulders as if her skin no longer fit. "He needs me and I do love him, but I thought Hope was going to be my biggest responsibility."

"He may not stay so childlike if we can get him healthier. Wait until you talk to his doctor before you fear the worst."

"I'm caught between my father, who barely knows me, and my daughter, who's bright enough to notice everyone in this town staring at her, wondering about her. I can't take her home and leave him like this, and I'm wondering if taking him from the place he knows would be wise."

"No one will hurt Hope." It'd happen over his dead body.

She looked at him as if she couldn't believe he was so naive. "You can stop it?"

"I'll do what I can. She's a little girl. No one would hurt her."

"Not on purpose," she said, "but people are cruel without thinking. I learned that before I left."

"You have to tell Leo about Hope."

"How can I? He thought I was his mother."

Van held very still. For the first time, they were talking, not fencing. "He seemed clearer after you talked for a while."

"I babbled. I just want to know what happened."

"I never got him to talk about anything except your mother or the house getting robbed."

She twisted her mouth. "I hate seeing him like that. And you were his son for a long time."

"If I'd ignored what he wanted and stayed in touch, maybe he wouldn't be in this shape."

She looked up. "It's not your fault. After the divorce, we weren't really family anymore." She stared at her father's cup. "But what changed him?"

"The same thing that changed us all."

She licked her lips, so dry they were cracking. "My life wasn't my own. There was the investigation, and even after that pig took the plea agreement, I felt everyone staring at me. All the time. You, barely able to share breathing space. My father, fighting to look me in the eye. Living here was like struggling each day through a thick bubble. Then, when I learned Hope was coming, I had to leave."

"Because you felt freer elsewhere?"

"Everything was easier where no one knew anything about me." She pulled the lid off her father's cup. "I'd better get water."

"It's over here." The nurses had shown him a machine that dispensed ice and water yesterday. He took the cup.

"You've got to stop helping me, Van. My family isn't your problem."

He filled the cup, anyway. "I let you down then, and I still don't know what I'm doing, but I want to do the right thing for you and me this time, Cass."

"Stop calling me that."

He took her arm. "And for Hope." If she asked what he meant, he was sunk. But they had to start somewhere. "I'm sorry for crowding you. Freedom, back in Washington, must look good." He handed her the cup. "I'll go away if you say that's what you really want." He waited until she faced him. "But I don't believe you do."

She didn't take a second to think. "You're wrong." She meant it. Her tone was all relief. He felt sick. Offering her hand, she was Hope greeting Beth this morning. "And thank you again for everything you did for Dad—and the house. Of course, I can't repay you."

"You just did. You made me believe I'm a stranger to you." Funny—she'd been saying it for almost twenty-four hours. "I should have believed you last night."

CHAPTER SIX

A STRANGER? Van had been her only lover, the man she'd hoped to have children with. The man she hadn't trusted to love her. And as he walked away, straight and masculine in jeans and a black sweater, he was more the man she'd loved than he'd ever been.

She could remember watching him across the skating rink, wanting him as if they hadn't made love just moments before they'd come to skate. She'd been so proud to be his wife. Her friends had lusted for his lean, lanky frame, and they'd told her in high school she just liked him because he was an older guy and because her father liked him so much.

She knew the day he'd finally opened his eyes and seen her. It had been the Christmas season then, too. Van and her father had spent a week with the bank's auditors. She'd made them a late dinner, and she'd served them both. After she'd squeezed her father's shoulder, filling his glass with tea, it had been natural to do the same for Van.

He'd caught her hand as if it had burned him, and he'd looked into her eyes with the awareness she'd dreamed of seeing. Later that night, he'd met her under the mistletoe. That had been their beginning.

She wrapped her arms around her waist.

Saying goodbye again hurt unbearably.

"Mrs. Haddon?"

How appropriate that someone should call her that now, after five years. She turned to meet the man coming down the hall. "Dr. Baxter," she said. His face was vaguely familiar, but she had to read his name badge. "My name is Warne. Cassie Warne."

"Call me Lang. I remember you, Cassie. Let's talk about your father."

Ah, the truth at last, in plain language, instead of couched carefully to keep from hurting her. She'd faced all kinds of truth, but she dreaded hearing what the future held for her father. Without thinking, she glanced over her shoulder for Van.

HE WENT HOME and tried to work. He had his own problems—a client's bank account that had flattened over the past year, two major clients who were as stunned as he that he'd made a wrong choice on their behalves, and new business he was in the middle of recruiting.

About three o'clock, he realized he'd stranded Cassie at the hospital without transportation. He thought about calling, but she'd convinced him it was sick to be so Johnny-on-the-spot. He'd rather drive back to the hospital. If she'd already left, he'd look in on Leo.

Before he went, he made a few calls, including one to answer questions for a prospective customer. While he glanced at the clock he found Hope creeping into his mind. How was she doing with Beth, a relative stranger? He didn't call.

None of his business.

Back at the hospital, he ran into Lang Baxter outside the break room on Leo's floor.

"How's the patient?" Van asked.

"Better. His daughter's worked a couple of miracles. They were talking about her mother when I last checked in. Let me say they were reminiscing about Victoria. I think Leo may come back some, once he's home in familiar surroundings."

Van nodded, aware at last that he had been a temporary Band-Aid for Leo. "That's a big improvement."

"More than I hoped for." Lang dug a pack of gum from his pocket and offered it.

"No, thanks."

"You didn't tell me Cassie'd dumped your name."

Lang's curiosity was a bucket of cold water. Their footsteps echoed on the white-and-black tile as Van got a grip on anger that surprised him. "You didn't say that to her?"

"I called her Mrs. Haddon at first. She didn't recognize me." He unwrapped his gum and popped it into his mouth. "What happened? Did she blame you for not being home that time—"

Good God. She'd been right about living in a town where everyone took a proprietary interest.

"Don't talk to her about that."

"I won't, but it's been a long time. No one ever understood why she left."

This conversation again. He turned, stopping the doctor. "I appreciate your care for Leo."

"Van, I'm sorry. I just asked because we couldn't figure out why she disappeared."

"No one needs to understand. It isn't anyone else's business." Even asking might hurt Cassie.

He turned and there she was, at her father's open door with his cup in her hand again. She stared from him to the doctor, her face flushed, a blotch of red on each high cheekbone.

"He wants more water," she said, and brushed past both of them.

"Oh, man. I'd better apologize," Lang said. "My wife calls me a gossip all the time. I thought she was nuts."

He went after Cassie. Van almost followed, but

he was a new man, the one she wanted. He left her to deal with Lang on her own and he went to visit her father. Leo looked up from his bed.

"Van, I'm feeling a little better this morning."

Van managed not to check his watch. Time passing wasn't as important as knowing the faces of the people who loved you. "I'm glad. You think seeing Cassie did the trick?"

"I never thought she'd come. How did she know where I was?"

"I called her. You had her phone number."

"I always kept it. She didn't want me to call, but I kept thinking who knew when I might need to?"

"You should have called one of us a long time ago."

"Yeah—I've got a little pneumonia." Leo breathed, as if he were testing his lung capacity. "But the doctor says I'm not going to die like Victoria."

Van glossed over the mention of Victoria. No need to dwell on hurtful memories. "When do you get to go home?"

"In a few days," Cassie said behind him. "Lang says he needs to stay until his lungs are clear."

"Good." Van expected her to be angry, but she looked empty. "I came back because I remembered I'd left you without a ride home."

"I can take a cab," she said.

"One of the two in town?"

"There are two now?" she asked, a brittle laugh in her voice.

"Are you two getting back together?"

"No, Dad." She lowered her head to hide behind her hair, an old habit.

"Van's a good guy."

"He always was." She set her father's water on the tray beside him. "But I don't live here anymore, and it's a long way to Washington."

"I live here, Cass."

She didn't answer, but Leo sounded so calm, so much like his old self, Van felt as if he were intruding. They didn't need him now. He reached for the door just as a nurse brought in a tray of bad-smelling food.

"Dinnertime, Mr. Warne."

"Cassie, I'll be out here."

"It smells like the stuff I used to feed my cat," Leo said.

He might have lost his memory and his manners, but his spunk was coming back.

"Wait, Van."

Cassie's voice startled them. He turned. "What's wrong?"

She nodded at the nurse. "Dad, we'll be back in just a second."

"Don't go too far, Cass."

"I won't. Eat a little of your dinner."

He eyed it with distaste. The nurse popped all the lids. "Cat food, huh? Eat enough and maybe you'll get strong as a cat and we'll be able to let you go home."

"All right, but as I recall, the Constitution forbids cruel and unusual punishment."

Van held the door for Cassie. She touched his waist with her hand, only to pull him with her, but his muscles twitched at the shock of the contact.

"It's what she said about Dad going home," Cassie said.

"You don't want him there?"

"Will you listen before you jump to conclusions? Obviously, I want him to come home and get better, and then I'll have to figure out what to do for the future. But first, I have to tell him about Hope."

"Do you need help?" He must be some kind of a fool.

"I know I told you to go away, but you were the only one who could talk him off that bridge." She looked down, but then brushed his arm, the way she used to when she was too young and too shy to admit she was attracted to him. "Tom came by today and told me what happened that night. I didn't realize how bad he was."

"It's all right. Don't thank me again." He moved away so she couldn't touch him, either. "I love him, too."

She clearly decided to get to the point. "I'm afraid if I tell Dad about Hope, he'll get worse again."

"I'll stay." And he'd try not to feel like her knight in shining armor. He peered at her father through the small glass slit in the door. "What did Lang say about his condition?"

"They ran all kinds of scans and blood work. He's not sure if it's early dementia or Alzheimer's." The rest poured out. "The compulsive behavior is like I read—some sort of comfort—but Dad's already improved today. Lang thinks that'll continue as long as I'm around and Dad can stay in the house." Her voice cracked.

Despite the fact that he was just an ox, he put his arm around her. She leaned, enough to reassure him he wasn't forcing comfort on her.

"It's just that he's been so afraid of this, ever since his mother died."

"It might not be that bad. Wait for the tests to come back. He was in such bad shape he might recover dramatically with a steady diet of good food and care."

"Lang said that, too."

"What else?"

"That we can try several medications, that I might want to get a nurse in later."

He tightened his arm. She didn't want to stay

here. Of course, home nurses probably worked in Washington, too. "Don't worry about that yet. He'll improve."

"Thanks, Van." Her soft face meant more than her words. "I've been kind of nuts since I got here, and I'm sorry. I'm not just saying that to persuade you, but will you come back in with me in case he needs you?"

He nodded and then followed her back into the room, cautioning himself to stay out of their family matters unless Leo actually wanted him.

The nurse patted Cassie's shoulder. "He's doing better with each hour," she said on her way out.

"I hope so."

Leo looked up from a dish of potato soup. "I could use a steak. Remember the steaks at Ellen's, Van?" He waved Cassie back into her chair with a drippy spoon. "We used to treat our clients." He grinned. "Or maybe the bank was treating us. Either way, those were meals I'll always remember."

"Dad," Cassie said, "I need to tell you about someone who'll be at home when we go back."

"Van, you mean? I remember Van. I'm not totally—" He twirled the spoon in a circle next to his temple.

Cassie reached up to clean soup that had dribbled onto his shoulder. "Not Van. Remember he and I were divorced several years ago."

"Now that was a mistake."

"Dad, can you let me talk? Will you listen to me?"

"I'm listening." He took more soup. "Someone else is at our house. Not a new guy?"

She shook her head, scrunching the folds of his sheets in her fists. "I have a daughter, Dad. A little girl named Hope."

His mouth opened and the spoon slipped out of his fingers and clattered to the tray. He stared from her to Van.

"You had a—you—neither of you told me?"

Naturally, he assumed Van was Hope's father. His troubled mind didn't allow him to think Cassie might have met someone else. She swung around to stare at Van. He went closer, naturally protective of her. Leo wasn't thrilled they might have had a child. How would he react—more importantly, how would he treat Cassie—when she told him the whole truth?

"Go on," Leo said.

Cassie turned back to her father. "Dad, she's not—I mean Van's not—" She stood. "Hope—"

"Is so young she doesn't understand about me and the divorce."

Cassie spun back to him, upset. Van shook his head. She'd asked him to help. This was the best he could do. He wouldn't let her father hurt her again. And if she could choose what to tell Leo, she wouldn't want him to suffer, thinking that animal had left her with a child.

Or so he told himself.

Maybe he didn't want anyone to know.

Breathing heavily, Cassie stared at him, anger glittering in her eyes, but it dissipated when she looked at her father.

"This is easier," Van said.

"I don't like it."

"You're the one who said it wasn't the worst thing people could think. Especially your father."

"What's going on?" Leo asked. "What are you two talking about?"

Cassie closed her eyes and then opened them. She seemed to reach her decision with an effort. "We haven't told Hope about Van, so I don't want you to tell her, either, Dad. I'll explain when she's old enough to get it."

"I'm pretty old," Leo said.

"You see everything in black and white. Hope is a shades-of-gray situation for Van and me. She was born after the divorce. She's never met Van."

"I can't believe you'd ignore your own child," Leo said to Van.

This was the price he'd pay for protecting Cassie. He could only stare his accusers down, starting with her father. "I was wrong," he said. He'd been wrong to give up.

"Van, I need some water. Come with me."

They were barely outside the door when she grabbed him by the shirt. "What the hell are we thinking?"

How much he liked the warmth of her hand against his stomach. "That he might not be able to deal with the truth. That he might accidentally tell someone else and then it'd be all over town." Temper flared in her eyes. "Not," he said, "because anyone here would blame you or Hope for what happened, but they'd ply you and Leo with sympathy. No one knows why you left or Leo became a hermit. Hope is a perfect doorway into your lives."

"My daughter is not a conversation starter." She pulled him even closer, barely glancing at the orderly who eyed her rough hand on his shirt. "I'm thinking of Trey Lockwood and the people who handle your business at the bank and your nephew, Eli. How many of them are going to believe you're the kind of man who'd let me walk away, pregnant? Who wouldn't try to find out the truth?"

"I didn't," he said, his shame a suit of nails.

She closed her mouth, breathing hard. She dismissed his bitter confession with an even more painful it-doesn't-matter gesture. "Stop trying to manage my life, Van. I thought you realized—"

"I understand everything you've said to me, but it's better that people think I'm her father. You know it."

She did, but she obviously didn't like it. "Not my father. Do you think he'll suddenly get well enough to hear the truth? Who knows what makes sense to him? Or what he even understands, but I can't—I won't—lie to him. He is still my father—and Van, he loves you."

He backed into the old-fashioned textured brick wall and she had to follow. She let go of his shirt, and he stared over her head, down the sunlit hall, giving them both time to calm down.

"Point taken. I'll explain. I'll say whatever you want. I was just trying to make sure nothing more hurt him or you or Hope. If you'd seen him on that bridge…"

"You decided for all of us, and I'm not sure if he'd even see why you lied."

"Why don't we let it go for now? We can explain after he comes home."

"We?" She turned away from him and pressed her head to the cool mint paint on the wall. "I don't know if you did this because you're ashamed a rapist made your wife pregnant or you just can't leave me alone, but my door is closed to you, Van." She took one deliberate step back, walking away again. "I was wrong to ask you for help." She turned toward her father's room. "I'll take a cab home."

They'd scarcely noticed four nurses who bent over their clipboards and loose pages, and in one case, a tray of medication.

Van had barely spared them a thought—the hope they'd be discreet—because he had a feeling Cassie was right. He told himself to get over her once and for all. He could pretend he'd finally stepped out of the limbo her divorce had exiled him to for five years.

He straightened his shirt, tucked it back into his waistband and strolled toward the elevator.

Why had he told Leo Warne that Hope was his child?

"ARE YOU ANGRY that Van told me about your daughter?"

"No, Dad. You need to eat your dinner." Which looked much like lunch. "Aren't you hungry?"

"Try a bite of that and see if you could choke it down. Even the pudding tastes like those fake potato flakes."

"If you gain a little weight you might get to come home. Have you been forgetting to eat?"

"My memory isn't what it was, but stop trying to change the subject. Van wanted me to know about his child. You're lucky he's not mad at you."

She stirred tonight's soup. "Try this."

"I don't say that to hurt you, but any man would resent a woman who didn't tell him about his own baby. You kept her a secret."

She shook her head, sweeping her hair behind her ear. "I didn't want anyone to know about Hope."

He was distracted enough to eat without arguing. "None of this makes sense to me."

"To me, either, Dad. We're in for a confusing time."

"Huh?"

"Getting you well, deciding what to do next." She couldn't help it. She still hoped they wouldn't have to stay in Honesty.

He breezed over the subject. "When do I get to see her?"

"As soon as you're well enough."

"Is she like you?"

"I guess." She'd been so grateful to look down on her newborn's face and recognize her own features.

"You're like my mother. I don't think I noticed that before. You were always so much your own person I never saw her in you until you walked in that door this morning."

"I was my own person?"

"Sure. You never took my advice. You wanted what you wanted, and you wouldn't listen to me about taking a degree that would bring you a good job in college—"

"You mean a degree that led to working in the bank?"

He nodded, shameless. Her sociology major had always troubled him. "And then you just had to marry Van. There'd never be anyone else for you. You'd loved Van all your life."

She looked up, but the afternoon sunlight through his wide window blinded her to everything except memories from the past. Her wedding day, Van looking as dazed as she with happiness. The conviction that she'd done exactly the right thing.

Unlike most brides, she'd never been afraid. Never doubted.

"I chose the right career, but you were right about getting married too young."

"Children never listen to parents. We're so easily taken for granted. Do you know how many times I watched you walk out of the house, annoyed with me for trying to caution you about a mistake, but you never even considered your decision might be wrong?"

She moved around the bed so she could see him. "Dad?" His eyes were clear. She'd swear he was back with her again.

"Like about leaving," he said. "You were wrong to go. You needed me and Van. We all let that beast rob us of everyone who mattered most."

His rising tone frightened her. "Don't get upset. You need to stay calm."

"I helped break up your marriage because I was ashamed," he said.

"No, Dad." With an arm around his shoulders,

she hugged him, careful not to knock the soup spoon from his hand.

As if remembering those days cost him too much, he returned to the refuge of his hazy present. "Now, now." He started eating again, one bite after another until most of his plate was empty. After he drained his juice, he wiped his mouth and set the cup carefully on the tray. "You have to face the facts. We all hurt. We all let each other down. Now that you've brought Van's little girl home, why couldn't you care for each other again?"

Cassie sank into a chair, as dazed as her father.

Soon he began to drift off. She moved the food tray away from him. He barely blinked as the tray's wheels squeaked.

The nurse returned to check his vitals. "I think he's asleep for the night, but you've done a good job. You've kept him alert and talkative all day. He's probably exhausted."

Cassie picked up her coat. "How long do you think it'll take to regulate his medication?"

"A few days. His lungs are already clearing. Dr. Baxter wants to run a few more tests to make sure we have a clear picture of the rest of his health issues." She whipped his bed into shape. "Why don't you go home and get some rest? You can come back tomorrow."

"I gave my cell number to the nurse at the

station. You already have my dad's home number?"

Her father muttered in his sleep.

"Van gave it to us yesterday. We'll get in touch if there's any change. Try not to worry, Cassie."

"Thanks."

"Knowing he can count on you will be your father's best medicine."

She meant it as comfort, but staying here, living in Honesty where her father could count on her—it was Cassie's worst fear.

In the lobby, she called a cab and then her father's house to say she was on her way.

"Take your time," Beth said. "We're making art."

"I can't wait to see." Anything that looked normal.

As she was paying the taxi driver in front of her house, Beth opened the door. Hope skipped onto the newly painted front porch.

"Hi, Mommy."

"Hey, baby." Cassie ran to meet her and scooped her up for a noisy kiss on both cheeks, but her little girl struggled down.

"Come look. I'm drawing flowers. And we made cookies."

"We burned some cookies." Beth held the door. "Your father's vintage oven defeated me."

"Vintage," Cassie said with a laugh. "I'll bet

that thing's over thirty years old. It always cooked a little hot."

"We had to clean it. Grampa had spidey webs." Hope leaned confidingly into her thigh.

"I don't think he enjoys cooking," Cassie said, trying not to imagine how he'd eaten in these past years.

"I'm going to get my flowers, Mommy."

"Okay."

Beth held her back at the door. "How is he?"

"Like one of those mystics who's starved himself into nothing but the slight will to live. And wisdom." But was he wise? She shrugged. "At least he thinks he knows best."

"A trait that afflicts my family, too. In the race to be right, Van and I have often acted more like combatants than siblings."

Cassie closed her eyes, the day's frustrations tempting her to shatter. "Some things about your brother haven't changed."

"What did he do?"

"He told my father Hope was ours, his and mine."

"Oh, man." Beth sank back. "I can see why you're upset, but if you think about it, how would your father recover from hearing the truth?"

"Did Van call you?"

She shook her head with perfect innocence.

"Dad's much better trying to put Van and me back together again."

"Oh, no."

"Mommy, are you broke?"

She hadn't heard Hope come back. "I'm just fine, sweetie. Why?"

"Someone wants to put you together again, like Humpty Dumpty in my book."

"I'm all back together." She gathered the treasure trove of drawings Hope clutched to her chest. "I can't wait to see these."

"Are you sure, Mommy?" She looked Cassie over, as if she expected chunks of her to fall off. Cassie wouldn't have been surprised. "You sounded mad."

"I'm not mad." Cassie took her hand and led her to the kitchen, the calmest place in her father's home now. Thanks to Van. She couldn't forget everything he'd done.

"But somethin's wrong," Hope said.

Cassie sat in a chair and pulled Hope into her lap. This was where letting Van inside her head got her.

"I was a little mad, but it doesn't mean anything. My dad wants me to do some stuff I don't want to."

"Like it was your bedtime?"

"That is one of your least favorite words." Cassie tried to smile at Beth, who followed them, obviously wondering if her brother had made her unwelcome.

"I like my bed at home, Mommy. When can we go back?"

"I'm not sure."

"I'm betting Mommy wishes she could head straight back this second." Beth straightened crayons and scented markers that lent the room a sticky sweet smell. "I'm sorry your grampa is sick, but I'm glad I get to keep you both with me a while."

Cassie lifted her head. "You think I want to run away?"

"Run away, Mommy? With me, though?" Overtired and easily distressed by unfamiliar emotions in new surroundings, Hope looked wary. She half climbed off Cassie's lap, up for an adventure, determined not to be left behind. "Where we going?"

Beth held the box of crayons close. "I didn't mean it was a habit," she said to Cassie.

"For five years I've never doubted every decision I made was for the best." Cassie wrapped an arm around Hope, holding on for dear life. "But I should have checked things here once in a while."

"You want honesty, Cass?" Beth set the box on the table, steeling herself to be thrown out. "What happened to you—well—" With her eyes on Hope, she broke off, but who could say anything more about that? "Your father and my brother should not have let you go, and you shouldn't have abandoned them. You all should have taken care of each other. You should have let us care for you."

"Beth." Honesty hurt. "I never meant to harm anyone. I was trying to—" She struggled for the right word, looking down on Hope's dark hair. "*S-u-r-v-i-v-e.*"

The letters hung in the air. What mother hadn't spelled something totally serious and hurtful to spare a child? Staring at Beth—Beth staring back—the incongruity got to Cassie.

Laughter bubbled out of her, startling and clean. Beth laughed, too, and then she swept around the table. Her hug felt sweet. Because they were together and time hadn't changed the fact that they loved each other.

Just like that, sharp and dear as her best memories, Cassie wanted Van back, too. She faced the truth. She was afraid of letting him back into her life, letting him matter.

But hadn't she cowered enough? Hadn't fear robbed her of five long years already?

CHAPTER SEVEN

CASSIE AWOKE gasping the next morning. The ceiling hanging over her head, familiar and yet so unexpected, brought her immediately home.

Van. His name whispered, a memory and a reason to feel guilty. A taunt? She lifted her left hand. For a month after she'd finally relegated her wedding rings to her jewelry box, their imprint had stayed on her finger. Gone now—as though they'd never been. As though Van had never been.

She threw back her sheets.

This house. Every time she opened her eyes here, memories, rich, and too dangerous, threw her back five years. Everyone knew you couldn't go home again. Home had moved on without her, and she belonged in Washington.

She twisted her hair into a chignon, slipped in a bobby pin, shivered in her tank and pajama pants and found one of her old high school sweatshirts.

Only it was Van's sweatshirt. Though he'd graduated eight years before her, she'd fished it out of his closet the first time he'd taken her to his house. She'd worn it with the pride of a barely-out-of-her-teens girl, distractedly in love.

She hesitated before pulling it over her head. But she wasn't a naive young thing anymore. She'd grown into a practical woman who chose to dress rather than freeze to death.

Her bedroom door burst open, and Hope whirled into the room.

"Time to get up, Mommy. I'm starwing, and I want to paint some pictures. Miss Beth said she'd bring paints today. Is my grampa coming home? Am I going to see Mr. Van again? He brings good food."

Cassie blinked. "Can I siphon off some of your energy?"

"Siphon?" Hope tilted her head, interested. "Whazzat?"

"Transferring some out of you, into me."

Hope grabbed her own pajama top, a fleecy rendition of Dora today. Still pink, naturally. "Nope. Might make a boo-boo. I'm really hungry, Mommy."

"What time is it? Did you make coffee, Hope?"

She giggled. "Funny, Mommy. I'm not old enough to drink coffee. I could make some, though," she said in all seriousness. "I know how 'cause I watch you."

Cassie grabbed her girl and they wrestled down the hall. "You'd better leave it to me for now."

They raced to the bottom of the stairs, and Hope landed with a thud on the hardwood floor just as someone knocked on the front door.

"Mmm," she said. "Maybe Mr. Van brought me more spaghetts."

"Don't get your hopes up, punkin'." Mr. Van wouldn't be back. In a display of perverseness that annoyed her, she was sorry she'd made herself so damnably clear to him. Suddenly, she'd learned to want what—whom—she couldn't have.

Hope yanked at the door until Cassie managed to undo the lock and the dead bolt. Beth stood outside, brandishing a white bag full of delectable aromas.

"Doughnuts from Hagenthaler's. I got the last bear claw, ladies, and I'm willing to fight you both for it."

"I can thumb wrestle," Hope said, pronouncing the *B*. She popped onto the porch. "Where's Mr. Van?"

"He's working in D.C. today," Beth said, and Cassie pretended not to notice her close glance.

"Izzat where our airoplane went, Mommy?"

"Where we rode the big bus."

"I didn't like that bus, Miss Beth. A man sat on my coat and he wouldn't get off."

"Till she thumped him with her purse," Cassie said, "purely by accident."

"I'm not 'posed to have accinents no more."

Beth laughed and spirited her booty into the house. "The better to avoid lawsuits, my dear."

"What kind of suit?"

"A grown-up kind that's hard to explain," Beth said. "Let's get some milk and coffee and feed Mommy before we send her to the hospital."

"Who's taking care of the lodge, Beth?"

"Aidan. He and Eli can handle it for a few days. He likes the change from his business. You never saw a man so proud to wield a toilet plunger."

Cassie made a face.

"I hope I hid my feelings about that a little more skillfully," Beth said.

"Maybe the grass is always greener." Cassie lifted the coffeemaker's lid.

"Have you been inspecting the grass around here?" Beth asked.

"Nope." Cassie borrowed her daughter's vehemence.

"Too bad. I'll do the coffee. You go dress to see your dad."

HER FATHER SEEMED to have worked the miracle of stealing energy from Hope. He quizzed Cassie on her life in Washington and warned her she was putting herself in danger, working at the shelter.

They went for a walk down the hall, with Cassie pushing his IV stand. With permission from his nurse, she treated him to soup and lime sherbet in the cafeteria. With touching excitement, he considered the break from eating in bed a treat.

Again, in the late afternoon, he tired. Instead of falling asleep, he suggested she might be missing her daughter.

"I would like to see her, and Beth probably has business to look after at the lodge."

"I've had a nice day with you," Leo said.

She kissed his forehead. "You need to come home soon, Dad."

"If I do, you won't leave?"

Her heart softened like the sherbet that had melted before he could finish it, with his conversation going at light speed. "How would you feel about coming home with me?"

His frown reminded her of Hope. "All the way to Washington?"

"It's not that far by plane. We'd take all your favorite stuff."

"I can't do that. I have responsibilities here. Obligations only I can take care of."

His voice broke at the end, and his anxiety filled the room. Cassie squeezed his hand. "You don't have to be afraid of anything. We'll work this out."

"Do you wonder how much time we have left together? I think I was really sick."

"Don't. You scare me." She hugged him again. "I'll bring your razor tomorrow, and maybe we could slip Hope in for a quick visit."

He grinned, looking reassuringly younger. "Cassie?"

She smiled back.

"I'm sorry about before. You know, when I couldn't look you in the eye."

"You see things pretty simply now."

"It's all through a haze, but I remember when I was cruel to you."

She leaned on her elbows on the bed rail. "It doesn't matter now. You're sorry. I'm sorry I didn't know you were sick. Let's call it even and be glad we both remembered in time that we love each other."

"Okay." He touched her shoulder. "Do me a favor."

"You're almost your old self, Dad."

"Listen to me while I'm feeling clear."

"I'm anxious about what you're going to ask."

"Because you already know what I want and you know I'm right."

"You're about to bring up Van."

He nodded. "You two split up. I told him to stay away from me. Our family fell apart, and none of us knew why."

"I knew."

"About me, but I think you were wrong about

Van. He was angry all right, but he kept trying to tell you he was angry at the man who…" His voice drifted a little. "The man who hurt you."

"I've heard all this from him."

"Try listening, only once, and then I'll leave you alone." He leaned back and exhaled, weariness settling on him like the haze he'd spoken about. "I'm sleepy."

"Good night, Dad."

"Uh-huh."

Whether he was asleep or not, he wasn't with her any longer. She backed out of the room and looked for Lang to tell him about her father's few moments of clarity.

"He's on rounds. He'll stop by Mr. Warne's room later, but I'll tell him for you. Try not to assume too much. His body is fighting back, but this could be a phase in his condition, too. Early on, you'd expect him to be clearer than he has been."

Nodding, Cassie stumbled toward the elevator. The nurse already assumed a more dire prognosis than she'd considered. She still hoped her father would get better. She hoped it enough to do him that favor.

VAN CAME OUT of the bank to a light snow muffling children's laughter from the Christmas tree lot on the square.

A balloon arose to the sound of a shout, sheer

joy only a child could feel. Over the trees, the red balloon floated, trailing a leash of dark green tinsel.

He hadn't thought about a tree for his own house. He tucked the receipt for his latest loan payment into his pocket. Having worked at the bank when he was just out of college, he knew that Jonathan Barr, who handled loans now, liked to feel superior to those who desperately needed them. Paying in person, with a total lack of concern, had become Van's petty revenge.

He'd like to be too busy to waste the fossil fuel, but an investment analyst was only as good as his last picks, and his errors eight months ago had given him more free time than he wanted.

No one could have worked harder to change that.

Those Christmas trees looked inviting. It'd be ridiculous to let Cassie's rejection turn him into a Scrooge.

He pushed his bare hands into his pockets and started across the street. A green mesh fence ran around the tree lot and he followed it to the parking area nearest the courthouse entrance.

A car's balking engine drew his attention. In a gray minivan, one of his neighbors, with a spectacular Douglas fir on her roof, was unsuccessfully trying to go home.

Van hesitated only a moment. He went over

and tapped on Lexie Taylor's window. She rolled it down, relief flooding her face.

"Do you think you could give me a jump, Van?"

"We could try that." He glanced into the back, where her son lazily kicked his boot-clad feet as he gnawed on a piece of teething toast. "You and Spence stay warm. I'll get my car."

"You're a lifesaver."

"Thanks." Gratitude beat suspicion any day of the year. He nosed his car as close to Lexie's engine as he could get it, and then took jumper cables from his trunk. After a couple of tries with the cables, he had to climb out and disappoint the mom-in-distress.

"Sorry, Lex. It's not working. I'm afraid we're going to drain my battery, too, and we'll both be stranded. Why don't I give you a ride home, and maybe Sam can get you a replacement battery?"

"Sounds good, if you don't mind driving us." She opened the door, sliding her arms into her coat sleeves. "But you were going in to buy your tree. We can wait."

He shook his head. "Let's move yours to my roof. You can't leave it sitting here. Spence needs his tree at home."

"Well, it cost enough that I'm reluctant to abandon it," she said.

"You transfer Spence and the car seat, since I

don't know how to hook them up, and I'll take care of the tree."

He undid the cables and backed the car into a space. Then he took her tree down while she moved the car seat across. He finished the tree about the time Lexie was leaning in to put Spence back in his car seat, laughing at a mother-son game that involved kissing and cradling of faces.

Grinning, wondering what it was like to be part of such a family, he straightened to find himself staring into Cassie's bewildered eyes. Hand in hand with her, Hope jumped as she saw him, too.

"Lookie, Mr. Van, we're buying a tree for my grampa."

He couldn't restrain a wary glance toward Lexie, who'd been a few years behind Cassie and Beth in school. She hadn't been too young to read about the rape and the trial. "Sounds like fun," he said.

"Come on, punkin'. Mr. Van's busy."

Before Lexie could raise her head, they were gone, swallowed by the fragrant evergreens and the laughter inside the fence, as if he'd imagined them.

"Van? Something wrong?"

He got a grip. "Not a thing. Spence all set?"

Lexie nodded. "And I'm freezing. You don't even have gloves."

He brushed the snow off his shoulders and out of his hair. "I missed the forecast."

"WAS THAT Mr. Van's girlfriend, Mommy?"

Exactly the disquieting question she had on her mind. The woman had tucked her little boy inside the car while Van tied down their tree. Working in tandem, they looked as if they were together. Used to being together.

"Where did you hear about girlfriends, missy?"

"I watch TV, you know."

"Apparently the wrong kind for your age. Want some cider?"

"Uh-uh." She shook her head. The hood on her coat shifted back and forth, mussing her silky hair.

"Hot chocolate?"

Hope slapped her mittened hands together. "Yummy."

"Let's indulge ourselves and buy a tree and pretend we're at home."

"What's hen-dulge?"

"Have something we really like. When I was a little girl, they sold tasty apple fritters along with the cocoa and cider." Who was she kidding? Not even a fritter would shave the edge off this dull, unexpected pain.

"I never had a apple critter."

"Fritter," Cassie said, visions of squirrels and chipmunks that hadn't been quick enough to hide for winter dancing in her head.

They bought a tree, which Cassie wrestled onto

the roof rack of their rented car while Hope shouted plentiful advice.

At home, she hauled the tree as far as the bay window in the living room. Then, while Hope stayed to admire it, Cassie plucked up her courage to visit the attic, where nothing was out of order. No paper towel stacks. No newspaper like the piles that had turned up beneath the master bath cabinets. Just the boxes and oddments she and her parents had stored over the years.

She found the ornaments and dragged the box downstairs. All the while, an image of Van, with that woman and little boy in his car, kept sneaking back into her mind. How many times had she asked him to stay away? And now was he putting a star on some other woman's tree?

That woman, laughing, had been grateful to him.

"Mommy, you look sad."

"What?" She brushed off Hope's concern. "I'm just avoiding the untangling-of-the-lights ritual."

Hope giggled. Together, they opened the box. Together, they decorated the tree, Hope doing the bottom while Cassie covered the top. Finally, Cassie lifted Hope, who managed to maneuver the star onto its place of honor.

"Can I plug in the lights, Mommy?"

"Maybe I should." They hadn't yet mastered

the concept of keeping tiny fingers from between the plug and the socket. "You keep an eye out for any bulbs that don't work."

Miraculously, the tree lit up.

"Let's open the curtains," Hope said, and again Cassie lifted her so she could push the drapes away from the living room window. Dust sifted down on them, and they raced to the kitchen to get water and take turns washing each other's faces.

"Time for dinner," Cassie finally said. "It got dark when I wasn't looking."

"Not bedtime."

"Pretty soon."

Hope yawned over their soup and sandwiches. Afterward, Cassie ran her a warm bubble bath, and then they turned to a stack of books.

At last, Cassie sang Hope's favorite good-night songs and traded "lights off" for a reading of *How the Grinch Stole Christmas.*

Hope was asleep before the sleigh reached Whoville.

Cassie eased the bedroom door shut and then went back downstairs to clean the kitchen. Running hot water into the sink, she peered through the window at the sky.

The view had changed since she'd moved away. New trees branched against a blue velvet night, pressing bony fingers into puffy, moonlit clouds.

Cassie plunged her hands into the bubbly water. She'd always preferred washing dishes by hand. It was her quiet time, her few free moments to contemplate the world. Tonight, freedom didn't sit well.

She'd lost her place in Honesty. The sky had changed. Her father had become a stranger. Van had insisted he didn't believe they were over, but he'd looked happy with that other woman.

Tsking, like her mother before her, Cassie slid dishes beneath the water. He might have been helping, just the way he'd insisted on helping her and Hope since she'd come back.

He'd always been a guy who needed to do something. He hadn't said "I love you" the first year they'd dated, but he'd washed her car and changed the oil and wipers, and shown up each Tuesday just to haul her garbage down the five flights of stairs from her apartment for pickup.

His first "I love you" had sounded more like a question.

The image of him asking someone else flashed through her mind.

She'd finished the plates when footsteps raced across the attic above her head.

A glass slipped. She swore but caught it just in time, and then backed up, holding it like a weapon. Crazy.

She set the glass on the counter and grabbed her mother's rolling pin before she lit out on tiptoes for the stairs.

The footsteps above raced back, almost even with her head. Something fell over up there. Another clatter followed. An intruder tripping over whatever he'd run into?

Common sense told her those footsteps were too fast. They even sounded scratchy. An animal had to be in the attic, but she'd just been up there. She'd seen no openings other than the dormer windows, close enough to the trees to provide an entrance for a human.

She'd moved some boxes. Maybe she'd somehow unblocked an opening for an animal.

Either way. She grabbed her cell phone and hurried to Hope's room, which had once been her playroom. She eased inside and locked the door.

"What's wrong, Mommy?"

"Are you awake?"

"Gonna read more?"

"Sure. Let me just make a call." She slipped to the window and checked the lock, then went to the bathroom. "I have to go in here a second," she said. "Choose a book."

"Okay." Hope rolled out of bed like a big drop of water, and then crawled across the rug to the bookshelf that still held most of Cassie's childhood books.

Cassie tripped over a wet towel and Hope's discarded clothes. She dialed the police.

"Honesty Police Department. Monica James," the dispatcher answered.

"Monica." They'd been in the same French class. "This is Cassie Warne. I think there's an animal in my dad's house." She gave the address.

"What kind of animal?"

"I don't know." She hesitated, not wanting to tell anyone about Hope, but she had to explain she had a child in the house. "The thing is, it could be a person—I just don't think so, and I didn't want to scare my daughter, so I thought I'd call the police. If you want to send Animal Control, that's fine, but we're locked in a bedroom until I'm sure what's going on."

"Maybe I'll send a patrolman and a crew from Animal Control. You've heard no voices?"

"No—just really fast feet."

"You know, the squirrels can't find much food in this weather. You're probably fine. Want to hold the line until someone comes?"

"No, thanks. My daughter hasn't heard anything yet, and we'll be reading until they arrive."

"I'm not supposed to let you hang up if there's any question in your mind about a human intruder."

"Do you mind if I just leave the phone on? I'll set it beside us."

"That's fine. When the car arrives, let me know."

"Thanks, Monica. I appreciate your help."

"Sure, Cassie. That's what we're here for. I'm betting on a four-footed visitor."

The other kind couldn't happen twice to one person? "Me, too."

Hope had turned on the tiny lamp they'd set up beside her bed. She looked up, a glow from the purple shade on her face, a book about mining moon cheese on her lap. "Mommy, who are you calling from the bathroom?"

So much for subtlety. Cassie crossed to the bed. "An old friend, sweetie. Scoot over, and I'll read to you." She set the phone on the nightstand. "You picked one of my favorites."

Hope held it up, open to a picture of a backhoe dragging cheese off the moon's surface. "You wrote your name. Miss Tawny, at my school, says I'm not 'posed to write my name in books."

"We all do things we're not supposed to sometimes. Let's open her up at the first page and see what else I did."

They'd reached the backhoe when blue lights flashed onto the faded yellow wall paint.

Hope dropped the book. "What's that?" She scrambled to her knees and then to the window, with Cassie tugging her back by her shirttail.

"I think there's an animal in the attic. The police and some other people are coming to find out."

"Police?" Hope looked scared. "I don't want them here in my grampa's house."

"Don't be afraid. I'll talk to them. And you know, the police are the good guys."

"I guess, but I don't like that bad man we saw the last time we saw police."

"They only came to help us with him." Standing, Cassie peeked through the blinds. "These things are dusty, too. We still have a lot of cleaning to do for your grampa."

"You're not scared?"

"Nope." Cassie smiled with total assurance. She and Hope had spent so much time together— alone—that lying to her daughter, even for her own good, rarely worked. Thank God they both believed in honesty.

"Okay." Hope slid back under the sheets but then straightened again. "You're not going out there?"

"Not yet. We'll let the police and the animal people check everything out first."

Downstairs, someone pounded on the front door. She should have unlocked it. She glanced from Hope to their door.

"I'd better go now, sweetie."

"Lock my door, Mommy?" Hope asked, peeping out from beneath the flowered sheet.

"Oh, sweetie. Try not to be afraid. I'll lock it. Come let me show you how to unlock, too."

They had a demonstration, and then Hope zoomed back to bed. Cassie eased into the hall as the pounding downstairs grew more insistent.

She expected the police, and they were there, but Van was right in front of her, being yanked back by Sheriff Drake.

As soon as Van saw her, he pushed back to the front. "Cassie." He swept her with a searching glance. "Where's Hope?" For the first time, he said her name with care. With real concern—as if she mattered to him.

CHAPTER EIGHT

HE TOOK HER breath away.

"Hope's in her room," Cassie said.

The scratchy footsteps charged overhead again.

"Oh, yeah, that's a squirrel," Tom Drake said. "Maybe two."

"Racing," his deputy said.

But Van looked wary. "Can Hope hear that? It might scare her."

Cassie shouldn't have been surprised. Hope's curiosity charmed even strangers. She loved easily, with a kind heart. Who could resist her?

"You're right." Turning, Cassie ran back up the stairs, the men at her back, though Tom reached for her shirttail the way she'd grabbed at Hope's.

"What if it's not an animal, Cassie?"

"The way I've been charging up and down these stairs, if it were a burglar or anyone else who wanted to hurt us, he probably would have shown up."

"Where's the attic door?"

"Down by the bathroom. Be careful. You have to pull the door, and a ladder drops down, but the hinges must be rusty. It's hard to manage."

The sheriff and his deputy went on. Van stopped by Hope's room with her. His hand brushed her waist.

She stepped away from him and unlocked the door, mostly because she wanted his touch, and she was disconcerted to find she didn't feel as if she deserved to be protected.

"Everything's fine," she said as she walked into Hope's room. Her daughter yanked the sheets down from her two eyeballs staring like a Halloween toy.

"You're not the police, Mr. Van," Hope said. "Where'd you get the lights on your car?"

"That wasn't my car." Van eased down onto the end of the bed. Hope shoved the sheets down and crawled over the bedding on her knees.

Cassie watched them, bemused. She tried to remember Van with the woman and little guy in his car, but that image wouldn't come. He looked too right taking the book from her daughter's hand.

"Hey, look, this must have been your mom's. There's her name."

"She wrote in it." Hope's disapproval dropped her voice low. "With a purple crayon."

He half hid a smile, just like a father. Cassie turned away and drew up the dusty blind, but when the dust settled, she saw all three of them reflected in the glass. A family. Almost.

She dropped the blind.

"You okay, Cassie?"

"Hmm?" Suddenly, she wanted to ask him about that woman and her son.

"Read to me, Mr. Van."

He waited for Cassie to answer. Finally, she tried to smile at him. He turned his head slightly, frowning. She knew the look. He knew she was hiding something. She smiled at her daughter.

"Let me fix this messy bed," Cassie said.

He picked up Hope and moved to the rocker, which creaked as he sat. "Is this okay?"

"It was my grandmother's. It'll either last with you or break for good."

She'd said more than she meant to, all but comparing the chair to their relationship. Van's smile asked her what was going on. She closed her eyes and breathed, trying to gather herself.

"Mr. Van, my book."

Cassie busied herself making the bed. So what if her father had asked her to give Van a second chance? Beth's speculations about his feelings didn't mean anything, either—except she had to wonder why Beth wouldn't have mentioned another woman.

She'd never trust Van to love anyone she loved—or her again.

Yet a still voice at the back of her mind—the voice that refused to lie—asked why she felt safer with Van in the house.

After she finished making the bed, she moved to the bathroom to pick up the towel and wet clothes. Overhead, tiny feet and bigger ones chased each other. Something scraped, and Cassie leaned around the bathroom door to smile at Hope, who grinned and immediately turned her attention back to Van.

All the while, Van read about mining cheese on the moon and never knew he was altering her feelings toward that book. Would she ever read it again without hearing his husky voice instead of her own?

Several grunts preceded a shout and something slammed—a door, a window.

"I'm going upstairs to see what's happening with the squirrels," she said.

At the same time, a knock came at the door. She practically ran to open it. Tom lifted his hat, like a sheriff in an old movie. Cassie finally laughed out loud.

"Hysteria?" he asked.

"A little." She pulled the door wider. "Come. The party's in here."

"Not for the family of squirrels my men have

just given up trying to catch. The Animal Control truck just pulled up." He nodded at Van. "Everything okay with you all now?"

"I think I'll add a dead bolt downstairs and check all the window locks." He tucked Hope's head beneath his chin as if he'd held her every night of her life. "And tomorrow I'm calling someone to trim those trees back."

Cassie's smile faded. Van had shown up years too late to save her.

"The trees are my responsibility," she said.

That woman this afternoon had shaken her. She and Van had seemed close. For the smallest frame of time after she'd talked to Beth and her father, Cassie had imagined she might find something of her old love with Van.

That was crazy.

"Thanks, Tom. I'll walk you out."

"I'll do that," Van said.

Good idea. It took him out of her daughter's room to more neutral ground, where visions of a made-up family might not dance in her head.

"You need to go back to sleep." Cassie took Hope's hand as she slid off Van's lap.

Her little girl was too slippery for her. She reached up for Van, who had no choice but to lean down and let her put her arms around him. "Thanks for reading to me." She hugged him so tight her feet came off the floor. "I wasn't scared."

"You're awfully brave," he said. "But I liked reading. That's a pretty good story."

"Come on, Hope."

She must have been tired. She climbed into bed and snuggled deep. Cassie kissed her temple and then ushered both men into the hall.

"She's a good kid," Tom said.

"I think so, too." He said nothing more, and she was too tired to care what he thought—or wondered—about Hope's possible father.

VAN MET the Animal Control officer at the door. Cassie had walked Tom down to his cruiser. "How long do you think you'll be?" he asked the officer, an old acquaintance.

"At least an hour, usually. Why?"

"I want to change the lock on this door."

He shook his head. "Because of animal infestation?"

"We thought it might be human. I'm changing the locks so I can sleep tonight."

"In that case, we'll take our time." With compassion, the other man punched Van's forearm.

Van met Cassie on the sidewalk, grabbing her as she slid on ice. "I'm running over to the Super-Center for a new lock and dead bolt."

She moved away, trying to hide the fact that she didn't want him to touch her, but he noticed. Ever since she'd opened the door, he'd longed to drag her into his arms until he was sure she was all right. How she couldn't feel his need…

"You think the squirrels stood on each other's heads with a set of lock-picking tools?"

"I expected you to laugh." He let his tone show he was too tired to argue. "But I'm going."

"It's late. I'd like to get to bed after these guys leave."

"It's not that late, and I won't even knock if they're gone when I come back."

"This doesn't make things better," she said.

He glanced up at the doorway, where the officer and a woman in a matching uniform were carrying traps inside. "I'm wasting time. Just let me do this, and I'll stay away."

"Because you have that woman I saw you with today?"

"Lexie? I *have* her? She's a friend."

"You buy Christmas trees with women who are just friends? That's not the way it works in Honesty."

Was she jealous? "Her car wouldn't start so we moved her tree and her son into mine, and I took them home." Cassie's doubt felt like two fists banging at his chest. "Why do you care?"

"I don't," she said, too quickly. "*Care* is a strong word, but why do you keep coming here if you and your 'friend' are buying Christmas trees together?"

"You heard me. Lexie bought the tree for her home, the one where she lives with her husband. I gave her and Spence a ride, but that's it. And even though I'm tired of you treating me as if I'm stalking you, I don't want you to think I'd be asking you to—" *Try again* would be two strong words. "To at least talk to me about what went wrong between us if I was involved with someone else."

"Why aren't you involved—" she rubbed her face "—with anyone else?"

Because no matter where he looked, he only saw her. And that was too much truth for her. "I've told you," he said. "I think time stopped for me when you walked out. In the back of my mind, I expected you'd come to your senses and see I didn't think you—that it was the rapist who bothered me—the thought of him—" He glimpsed Hope's window and put all thoughts of that monster out of his head. He'd cared about Hope, needed to see with his own eyes that she was safe. "Talk to me when I get back," he said. "I want to change the locks tonight."

He veered around her, looking over his shoulder at the window again. An extraordinarily mindful daughter, Hope had stayed in bed.

Or maybe like any child with mischief in her soul, she'd already worn herself out today and she'd fallen asleep once the danger had passed.

Van had only one thought. He wouldn't talk

tonight about the man who'd raped Cassie and fathered Hope, because nothing should poison the tender roots of his hard-fought affection for the child who should have been his.

CASSIE CLEANED the kitchen until it shone, believing Van about Lexie, but troubled by her own feelings. A light tap came at the front door. She braced herself and opened up for Van.

"Do you know where your father keeps his tools?" He seemed to find a point above and between her eyes too interesting to look away from.

"They were always in the garage. I'll look."

"I will."

"You don't have to worry about me. I've already been out there, and I didn't find more stashes of anything odd."

Van's expression softened.

"I love him, Van."

"I know."

"I'm sorry about the past five years. And he's really anxious to meet Hope. Maybe I was wrong."

"To leave? I think you were." He turned away. She ached to reach for him, but she let him go.

While he was in the garage, the Animal Control officers brought down a squirrel family of three. One of the men paused on his way out. "I have some plywood in the truck. I'll come back and hammer in a temporary barrier."

"It's late," Cassie said, uneasy with everyone's helping hands. "I hate to trouble you."

"If I don't put up something, you're liable to call me back in the wee hours," he said. "There's a clean square in the dust in front of the hole. Someone must have uncovered the opening lately, maybe moving a box."

"Me," she said. "I thought I was tidying things while I was hunting for Christmas ornaments today."

"Yeah, these old houses. You try to get them in better shape, but you often uncover bigger problems."

"You have experience?" Cassie asked.

"I live in one a lot like this on the next street." His squirrel prisoner kicked up a fuss, reminding them he wasn't a natural cage-occupant. "Better get our little friend out of here."

Hope slept through Van wrestling with painted-over lock plates and the Animal Control officer hammering the squirrel door shut. After he finished and refused coffee for himself and his colleague, they all left.

Cassie felt too alone with Van.

He brought a lock into the kitchen. "Last door," he said. "Then I'd just like to check the ones on the windows."

"I have."

They stared at each other through thickened air.

"I'm mostly over it," she said, "but I'll never leave a window unlocked again."

"Do you admit that to everyone?" He knelt in front of the existing lock.

"Who needs to know?" She washed the counter again.

"I didn't," he said, "not really. But I'm glad you confided in me."

"I just didn't want you to make pointless rounds at the windows."

"I wish I'd been around that night to do it." He set the screwdriver in the painted screw's head and fought to turn it. "You'll never know how much—"

"I wished a long time, too, but that was futile and painful." She folded the tea towel into increasingly smaller squares. "A woman should be able to leave the shower window open to air out steam. It wasn't an invitation."

Van's head snapped up, but at last she saw his anger was directed at the man who'd hurt her. Not at her. "No one ever blamed you," he said.

"I'm the one who forgot to close that window."

"He's a criminal, and if he ever comes out of prison, I'll—"

"Do nothing." Cassie cut him off.

"What if he came back? Do you know how many nightmares—"

"Of course I do. I have them, too, but I don't

talk about them. I don't want you hurt, and I sure don't want you sharing a cell with him." She kept her own counsel about what she knew of that man. No news about him ever restored her sense of safety.

"You'd care about me?"

He must be out of his mind. "I always cared. I left because you couldn't care anymore."

"I wanted to kill him. Every time I looked at you or touched you, I dreamed of new ways to make him hurt."

"I can't." Until that moment, she hadn't known she couldn't talk about that night. Not with Van, not when she'd screamed his name in her head over and over. And been grateful he wasn't there.

The man had held a knife to her breast the entire time. A knife he might have used on Van.

She shook her head and saw herself as if in a dream. That was the way she'd dealt with the rape back then, acting as though it was happening to someone else. She'd felt like a stranger afterward.

Van stood and came to her, his eyes intent.

"What are you thinking? Tell me." He'd asked so many times before she'd left. She'd hated those words.

"That I don't want to relive that night again. I want to be back in my own body."

He took her arms. "What are you saying?"

"I convinced myself I couldn't feel, as if I were

floating above my own head, and I would be okay."

"You weren't."

"Your eyes scare me. You're so afraid for me."

"I was then, too, but tell me you aren't pretending again because I'm around."

She shook her head. "It's been five years since I've let anyone except Hope touch me for this long."

Immediately, he opened his hands, but she caught his wrists.

"Why are you changing my locks?" she asked. "Squirrels with lock-picking tools make me laugh, but no one else has a key."

"We don't know that. Your father might have given one to anybody. He might have dropped a key on the bridge that night." He went back to the door. "All the way around the lake tonight, staring at the lights on Tom's car, I wondered why I hadn't looked down. I thought someone had picked up the key, read about Leo in the paper and assumed the house was empty."

His glazed expression didn't belong to Van, her husband who'd been certain of every move he made, every decision he reached.

"The crazy thing was, your father gave me his keys at the hospital," he went on. "I used them to get in the house, but I was so afraid for you and Hope, I didn't remember having them."

"And Hope? What changed for you?"

"She's part of you." She knew him. He'd said it without thinking, without trying to make her think he'd changed.

She pulled out a chair and sat.

"You love her," he said. "Why are you stunned that I care about her?"

"I learned to love the idea of her because she was part of me, too. I'm not a bad person."

"A little misguided, sometimes."

She smiled, her mouth trembling.

He set the screwdriver on the floor. It glinted silver and rolled into a wrench, giving Cassie something to look at instead of Van. He knelt beside her.

"Don't." The past five years squeezed her so hard she couldn't breathe.

"If I'd been more insistent then, would you have stayed?" He took her hands.

Her heart betrayed her, beating too fast. Her mouth went dry. She'd felt the same the first time he'd looked at her as a woman and not just Leo Warne's daughter.

"Van, it's too late."

"Not 'it,' Cass. Either you and I have stopped caring for each other, or we can try to salvage something from the love we both felt."

His hands fascinated her. They looked the same, and hers did, too. After five years. "No one has touched me," she said. "I didn't think I could stand being touched."

"Am I familiar? Safe?"

She looked into his green eyes. Beautiful eyes she'd loved. Each morning when he woke, each evening when he came home to the house and the bed and the life they'd shared.

She shook her head. "Anything but safe."

"Why? I'll never hurt you."

"You might make me risk feeling again."

"Cassie?" He pulled her to him. His hands closed around her shoulders as if he were testing the feel of her. She couldn't move her own arms to hold him. Her heart lodged in her throat. She was choking.

Van didn't seem to notice. He pressed his mouth against her hair. She heard her name again, the barest whisper. She uttered a sound.

He backed up and opened his arms.

"I'm sorry. I didn't mean to force you." His shame was a palpable force that made her feel sick.

"No." She grabbed his wrist. "I'm just not used to—"

"I'll finish the locks and go."

"The one thing seeing you with your friend Lexie taught me was that I may not want you myself, but I don't want her or anyone else to have you." She had no shame.

His arms dropped to his sides. His mouth thinned. "What am I supposed to do?"

"Give me time? Even though I'm not being fair."

He shook his head.

"My father asked me to try, and your sister said you still care for me. Am I too late?"

Van climbed to his feet, slapping at the knees of his jeans. "When I need Leo and Beth to find me a date, I'll be in real trouble. As it is, I have a thing for you, even though you divorced me five years ago. That's as nutty as I want to be."

She froze, longing for an answer she could live with—an answer that would make them like any other man and woman.

"Maybe you should check on Hope," he said.

"Let me try again, Van." She started toward him, determined to make him see she might be ready.

He stopped her. "I'm not your last, best hope. I'm a man. I was your husband. I deserved more trust than you gave me then, and I won't be the one you settle for now."

"You misunderstand." And the thought of him leaving for good hurt so much, she ached for enough trust to ask him to stay. Those words refused to come.

"Even I have a little pride, and maybe you can't see that you aren't willing to need a man anymore."

Her foot inched to stomp, but she was a

grown woman. And that annoying voice in her head still insisted he might be right. She whirled, too flustered to care about being melodramatic. "Good night."

She stopped at the kitchen door, pointedly waiting for him to answer her like a civilized human being. The screwdriver scratched against metal.

Maybe she didn't care about civilized. Maybe she wanted him to help her forget she no longer knew how to be touched. She wrapped her arms around herself.

"I'm going up to take a shower. Lock up when you leave."

He grunted as an answer. She didn't tell him she was happier taking a shower tonight with him in the house. He didn't need to know the squirrel family had spooked her. But Van didn't leave while she was bathing.

She'd finished and was toweling her hair dry when she heard the front door open and close. She went to the hall as the dead bolt turned.

"I KNEW I'd get to meet you before you came home with us, Grampa."

A week after they'd arrived in Honesty, Hope addressed her grandfather from the bony discomfort of his lap. As usual, she'd seen someone who belonged to her in any way sitting, so she'd assumed he was meant to hold her.

"Punkin', don't swing your legs." Cassie feared Hope might break her father's.

For at least the third time, he protested. "She's fine. Let the girl be, Cass."

"I don't want her to hurt you."

"I'm not fragile."

Cassie folded a pair of his pajamas into the sports bag she'd dug out of her closet—a relic of her field hockey days. "You could gain a few pounds. Your doctor says so."

Behind her, the door opened. Van, of course.

"Mr. Van." Hope slipped to the floor and ran to swing on her new best friend's hand.

Her father clapped like a little boy. "Thank goodness you've come. My daughter's turned into a nag. She may drive me crazy before we get home."

Hope giggled, but Van looked stern. "That's not nice, Leo. Cassie just wants you to be healthy."

"So she can escape again."

"Dad." Cassie nodded at Hope, who'd already let go of Van to sort through her grandfather's shaving kit.

"Leave that stuff alone." Cassie redoubled her folding speed. "You'll cut yourself on a razor or something."

"Nothin' good, anyway." Hope gave the bag a little shove. "Mr. Van, are you my mommy's brother?"

He laughed too loud.

Cassie saw nothing funny. "I told you, Mr. Van is my friend." Like Lexie? She shook the thought from her head. "What say we stop at Mrs. Draper's diner for lunch? Lang says you can eat whatever you want. And, Hope, she makes homemade ice cream."

"Choplit?"

"The best."

"Okay. What are you gonna have, Grampa? Mr. Van can come, too."

While they planned their meal, Van began helping Cassie pack her father's things. He passed her a T-shirt.

She took it with less grace than his help warranted. "You could say you're busy."

He reached for another shirt, his mouth tilted in a wry smile. As he leaned toward her, he made her feel small—and safe. She had to defend herself against such temptation.

He nudged her with his elbow, entirely unaware of her turmoil. "I'm not intruding for once. Hope said I could come."

Cassie turned her head to hide a smile he had no business seeing.

"I think you should come, too," Cassie's father piped up. "You need to know Hope better, and I've missed you, too, Van. We need to get this family back on the right track."

CHAPTER NINE

AS CASSIE STARED at her father, appalled, Van grabbed the back of Leo's wheelchair. "What say I roll you two down for a soda? Hang on, Hope. If anyone sees you hitching a ride, we're busted."

"Mommy won't let anyone bust me."

Van laughed at her certainty. He'd bet "Mommy" would defend Hope with her last breath. He changed the subject before she became too curious about exactly who made up her family.

"Want anything, Cass?"

"An iron skillet to the head."

Leo peered over his shoulder. "What did you say? I couldn't hear you."

"I said by the time you get back, I'll have cleared your things off this bed." She stuffed his shaving kit in the bag. "And then we can go."

"Instead of eating at Mrs. Draper's diner, why don't I stop at that Posh place for takeout again, Cassie?"

"You don't have to do that, Van."

"I know I don't have to, but we can eat takeout at home. I care about Leo, and I'd like to see him settled and rested."

"I forget how close you were."

"So you don't mind?"

"I don't mind," Leo said, "and it's my house. Let's get that drink, son. I'm parched."

AFTER THEY ATE, Leo took Hope into the living room to color. Van helped Cassie with the dishes. Her father had insisted on real china.

"At least he's letting us wash it," Van said without thinking.

Cassie turned, a plate in her hands. "What do you mean?"

"Sorry. When I first came in the house, he'd used all the dishes and then started on paper ones, and they were all stacked in the dining room."

"Why?" Cassie wiped her hair away from her face, streaking her hair with soap suds.

He used a tea towel to blot up the foam. "I don't know. Sorry I mentioned it."

"Lang said he might fixate on behaviors that seem incomprehensible to me."

A high-pitched scream shattered the house.

"Hope." Cassie's voice poured terror into the silence.

Van ran ahead of her as Hope screamed again and again. In the living room she stood over her grandfather, who lay unconscious on a flower-strewn rug.

Van dropped to the floor and flipped his phone open.

"Wait." Cassie scooped Hope into one arm, at the same time grabbing a slip of paper from her back pocket. "Lang gave me his home number as well as his office and the hospital. Call him first."

In the back of his mind, Van wondered why the doctor was so solicitous. Idiotic. He checked for a pulse and found one. Leo seemed to be breathing steadily. He dialed the home number first.

A woman answered as Cassie shushed Hope, turning her head away from Leo's prostrate body.

"Lang Baxter," he said. "I need to talk to him."

She sighed. "Just a minute." She turned away from the phone. "Lang, it's for you. Again. How many times is this—"

"Baxter," the doctor said.

"This is Van Haddon. I'm over at Leo's. He's just passed out. He's breathing, and his pulse feels steady to me." He looked across the room. "Hope? Hope, honey, did Grampa say that he hurt anywhere before he fell down?"

She shook her head. "Make him better, Mr. Van."

"Did he say anything at all?" Van asked.

She shook her head, tears soaking the dark hair already plastered to her flushed cheeks.

"He said noth—" Leo's head moved to one side and then the other. Van tried to stop him, gently holding his head still. "He's waking up."

"A side effect of one of his medications is fainting."

"Should I get an ambulance?"

Lang hesitated only a second. "I'll come over. He's been miserable at the hospital."

"Thanks. Are you sure he'll be all right?"

"If I'm not, we'll call an ambulance after I examine him. Don't move him."

He hung up. "We're not supposed to move you, Leo. Do you mind lying here until Lang comes?"

Leo's eyes seemed to roll. He was searching for Cassie. "You won't send me back to the hospital?"

Cassie glanced at Van. He laid his hand on her shoulder, wishing he could give her more than inconsequential comfort.

"I'll try not to," she said, "but if Lang thinks you'll be better there…"

"He doesn't know anything."

Hope sank to the floor, leaning her head on her grandfather's chest. "I'll stay with you, no matter what. I never had a grampa before."

Cassie looked desperate. Van urged her to sit on the ottoman beside her father. He sat on the floor next to her and pulled Hope into his lap. "Better let your grampa get all the air he can."

Hope leaned against him, her head heavy, her chest quaking every second or so with a gaspy little cry.

"Do you want some water, Dad? That should be okay."

"No, sweetie. I don't want you to leave me, if you don't mind."

She nodded, her mouth tight, her eyes wet.

Minutes later, the doorbell rang. Van and Hope stood together. To his surprise, she took his hand, and they walked toward the hall. At the doorway, he glanced back at Cassie. She looked as frightened as Hope. His heart ached for her so intensely he rubbed his chest as he opened the door.

"Lang."

They shook hands, already moving toward the living room. Leo struggled to rise, but Lang urged him back. "Just a minute," he said. "Cassie, why don't you and Hope and Van give us a minute?"

They trooped out to the hall. Van shut the door and lifted Hope to his hip. At the same time, Cassie leaned her forehead against her daughter's and her shoulder pressed into Van's chest.

He put his other arm around her. "He'll be all right. Lang said this might be a side effect."

"Did he faint that first night?"

He had to shake his head. "But if it's the medication, he'll be fine."

Hope looped one arm around Van and one

around Cassie. "I don't like when grampas are sick."

"Neither do I," Cassie said.

"I don't like when moms and little girls are so upset." Van hugged them both. "I wish I could do the worrying for both of you."

He expected Cassie to wrench herself and Hope away from him, but she put her arm around his waist. He held his breath while the scent of her hair seduced him. The silky strands teased him. He longed to stroke his chin against the top of her head.

When the door opened again, they all stared at Lang, waiting for news. He grinned.

"He's fine, you three. Calm down. The man's not fragile. His vitals are all normal. He's had enough blood work he ought to be anemic, so I know there's no infection or disease. We'll lower the dose of his medication and see what happens from there. For the next week or so, don't leave him alone too long. He's not to drive at all."

"Okay," Cassie said.

Van wanted to move between her and Lang, protect her from anything else that could hurt.

"And don't let him walk anywhere alone." He opened the door again. "Van, help me get him upstairs."

He did. When he came down, Hope was coloring again, hunched over the ottoman. Cassie was pacing up and down the living room, her eyes wide.

"Let's go out for a coffee," he said.

She stopped, an immediate no forming in her eyes and on her lips.

"Please," he said, though he wasn't used to begging—even for Cassie's time.

"Hope's bedtime…"

"I'll call Beth."

"I hate to leave Dad."

"He'll be fine. Beth's been raising Eli for twelve years. She has watchdog experience. She's equal to anything Hope or your father can come up with."

She smiled. Hope looked up. "I don't mind, Mommy. I like Miss Beth." She grinned at Van, a coconspirator.

Cassie acted as if she hadn't noticed. "Let me check on my father and get Hope into her pajamas."

"I'll call."

Beth agreed to come immediately. Lang came downstairs while Van was waiting for Cassie and Hope to come back. Van explained their plans.

"I'm worried about Cassie. She's tense, and I'd like to take her mind off things, but if you think Leo's in any danger…"

"None. He'll be better off without Cassie hovering over him."

"Ho-ver-ing?" Van said, enunciating each syllable.

"You know what I mean. Still protective after all these years?" Lang shrugged. "Cassie and Leo Warne are too careful around each other. She makes him nervous because she wants so badly for him to be well. He makes her anxious because she can't help analyzing each word and every one of his actions."

Because she wanted to leave Honesty, and she couldn't if her father wasn't able to take care of himself.

"They both have some things to make up to each other."

"I wish they would so they could get on with living."

It was a cliché that could change a man's life.

Cassie reappeared at the top of the stairs and Lang turned to her, giving further directions for her father's care. Van stared at them both.

Had she heard what Lang had said?

Did she realize he'd diagnosed all of them in one fell blow? She and Leo and he were all stranded in a triumvirate of detachment. Where once they'd been a family, they'd split apart without ever explaining themselves.

He'd tried to put Beth and Eli in Cassie and Leo's place. That hadn't worked. Cassie had replaced him and Leo with Hope, and she'd raised a loving, lovable daughter who'd already begun to capture his heart. Leo had embraced forgetfulness.

He had a feeling none of them had fully lived a single day since she'd left.

"Van, I'll be down in a second. Hope and I are going to say good-night to my father."

He nodded. Coffee, hell. He had to ask Cassie if she was willing to live again. He pulled on his own coat, struggling to make it fit as if he'd never worn it before.

Even if he forced Cassie to turn her back on him once and for all, living with all contact broken was better than this half-life he'd grown to hate.

"I'll go," Lang said, shaking Van's hand. "Call if you need anything else."

Van followed him onto the porch, into falling flakes of snow that glittered like diamonds in the streetlights.

"Thanks, Lang."

The other man raised his hand. His car pulled away, leaving a cloud of exhaust that slowly dissipated. Two houses down, a Santa stood inside a plastic globe that percolated snow over a chimney top. Up and down the street, icicle lights blinked on and off in a silent strobe.

Van pulled his collar close. Nights like this reminded him of moments he'd spent alone over the past five years. Happiness he'd thrown away because he hadn't fought to make Cassie believe in him.

She'd rejected his arguments before. He breathed in the cold air. She might reject him for the last time tonight, but she'd know he wanted to start over—with her and Hope. No guessing, no pretending he didn't understand she thought he'd let her down.

It was now or never, because neither he nor she nor Leo nor Hope had another five years to waste.

"LET'S NOT GO TOO FAR, Van." Second thoughts had started the moment she'd agreed to leave with him. "I don't need time away from my father."

"Everyone needs a break."

Some thread in his tone, a huskiness that sounded like a cold—or like his voice when they'd made love all those years ago—made her stare at him across the dark car. "What's wrong with you?"

"Something Lang said."

"About my father?" She settled her hands quietly in her lap. "Something he wants you to tell me?"

"Didn't you hear him, Cassie?"

"Every word he said to me." She frowned. His profile, sharp and unfamiliar, made her hug the car door. "Are you angry?"

"No."

He didn't say anything else. She let it go. "I can't face another argument today."

"Tonight," he said, and turned down a street she didn't know.

"Where are we going?"

"To my house. I'll make you coffee."

"I think of you in that old Victorian." They'd bought it just before the rape. It hadn't been habitable, then. They'd rented the small apartment that became her idea of hell and started restoring the house themselves. "What did you do with it?"

"I finished it."

"You live there?" Somehow, it seemed like a betrayal. That house, up on a hill with a guest house for her father should the need ever arise, had been the stuff of their future. Their dream of a future together. He'd lived their dream without her? "How did you do all the work?"

"I hired a lot of contractors."

All the same, she didn't want to see it. "Isn't there a coffee shop closer?"

"Yes."

"Let's go there."

"I'm not trying to force you, but I want to talk, and I'd rather not have an audience."

"No, Van." She put her hand on his arm. His muscles jumped. She felt them through his coat and his shirtsleeve. "I'm telling you I don't want to see it."

"That's something of an answer already," he said.

"To what?" He was scaring her. "You weren't even angry with me after the—attack."

He glanced at her, his eyes looking black in the car. "I didn't think you noticed."

"But you are angry now."

"Just determined. For once, you're going to hear me out. If you send me away this time, I'll stay gone."

Instinct brought a flip dismissal to her mouth. She pressed her fingertips to her lips before it escaped.

He passed through the square, turning right at the courthouse. The road opened onto a wide avenue of Christmas lights and deepening snow, red ribbons that glittered with ice, candy-cane light poles dressed in green velvet ribbons. People strolled past shops, fathers with daughters, mothers with their own moms, families with the children hopping between their parents' outstretched hands.

"Oh," she said.

"Santa's waiting in that little house at the end." He pointed, but she barely had time to see before they turned again and he found a parking spot.

"We always had to go to D.C. for shopping," she said.

"Honesty's growing, even when the folks

who've lived here since birth vote against expansion like this."

He opened his door and then came around to open hers, too. "It gives us a place to walk."

"Walk?"

"And talk."

"Sounds good." Walking would straighten out her thoughts and keep her from promising anything reckless. She didn't necessarily trust the Christmas-induced warmth of Honesty's new square.

They walked around the first building. "It looks like a movie set," she said, as they stepped into light that was almost like day.

"It's not real," he said. "The buildings are, and so are the sales going on inside, but the ambience works because it's what people want."

Where had her gloves gone? She tucked her hands into her pockets. "What are you trying to say?"

"We've put five years' worth of days between us because it was what you wanted, but your father and I haven't lived. Maybe it's different for you with Hope, but I've tried to make a home out of a house that was meant for you, and your father's made a mess out of the home you shared."

"Things," she said, "that we can fix for Dad."

"Your father needs the connection you had." He turned her suddenly, and she found herself inside a shop filled with knitted goods. Afghans, featuring Santas and reindeer, but also ducklings and building blocks. Hooded sweaters with mittens swinging from their empty sleeves.

Van walked straight to a set of cubbyholes filled with knit gloves. He chose a pair made of pale pink yarn. When he laid them in her nerveless hand, they were so light she hardly felt them.

"What's this?"

"Your favorite color." He covered her left hand with both of his and rubbed some warmth back into her skin. Warmth that traveled all through her body.

She shuddered. "Stop." And she pushed the gloves back at him.

He took them from where they'd stuck to the wool of his navy coat. Catching her hand, he tugged her with him and laid the gloves on the cashier's counter. "We'll take these."

He paid, while she fought heaviness that nailed her feet to the wide plank floor. Need sparked by his mere concern for her.

After he paid, she turned toward the door first. Outside, he caught her again and tried to put a glove on her hand.

"I'll do it." She didn't care for her own irascible tone. "What's happening?"

"You're upset because I can still make you want me."

"What?"

A woman walking by stared at her. "Cassie?"

"Hi." She didn't recognize the passerby. "Visiting my father."

With matching poor manners, Van wrapped his arm around her shoulder and suddenly, they were standing in the doorway of the next store down the street.

In the bay windows on either side, chocolates of every kind rested on red satin. It was like a brothel for desserts.

"I'm sorry ahead of time for taking advantage, Cassie."

He curled one finger beneath her chin and urged her head up. She saw mistletoe on a silver strand before his mouth grazed her chin. She breathed in—Van and chocolate and evergreen and the freshness of falling snow.

He kissed her cheek. His eyes were closed. His eyelashes, darker than his dark blond hair, tempted her lips. He pressed her face to his.

"Van," she whispered.

He reached her mouth. It was a chaste kiss, a touching only. But still a temptation, because his hands, just beneath her breasts in her open coat, stroked the way she'd always liked, teasing, making her want.

But his touch was light. She could have pushed him away. She could have stepped out of his arms.

She knew why he was being so gentle. He was thinking of that other man, the one who'd taken her with a knife, and Van didn't want to scare her.

His mouth lifted for a moment. He opened his eyes. Frustrated, she moved toward him and looped her arm around his neck, dragging him closer.

This time he kissed her the old way, the way of the first lovers and the way of the last who'll ever live. His mouth invited her into the past, and yet, he was different. He needed her, and his hunger was in the tilt of his head, his harsh breath, the desperate clasp of his hands.

"Wait," he said, pulling away.

A couple pushed past them, laughing.

Cassie closed her eyes, and then opened them to run out of the doorway with Van, into the cobbled road no car had ever dirtied. Beneath the bow-laden trees, darkness hid her embarrassment.

"Cass?"

"I don't know what to say."

"No one cares. It's Christmas. Everyone gives in to excess this time of year and I started it."

"Your voice…" She shivered. She'd awakened from dreams, hot and cold and sweating, hearing his voice, knowing she'd never feel his touch again.

"I want you," he said. "I never stopped. I just didn't want to hurt you, and I had a hard time believing any man touching you wouldn't hurt." He laughed, pulling at his own black gloves. "I finally said just what I meant all these years. We should have tried mistletoe first thing."

"It happened in July."

"Give us a chance to forget and move on, Cassie."

"I don't know if I can let you that close." She pressed her hands together, enjoying the soft yarn against her skin. "I haven't…there's been no one else since I left here."

"For me, either," Van said.

"I don't believe you." She hadn't been his first. She'd known the other women in town who'd been with Van. "You were always—"

"Because I loved you." His eyes ran over her, a moody brush of sensation that made her knees weak. She sat on a frozen bench.

"Cassie, there's snow." Van pulled her up and brushed the snow off. She sat again, hard. He made room for himself beside her.

She pressed her knees and her feet together and burrowed her hands into her pockets.

"What do you want to do?" Van asked.

"Go back to Washington, where it's safe." She remembered the man she'd fought at her shelter on her last day at home. "Where it's safer than here with you."

"I'll follow you this time."

"And your business?"

"I can bring it with me or deal with it later." He stared at the people streaming past them, their bags glittering, their laughter loud. "Although I should tell you I'm not quite as solvent these days."

"Are you in trouble?"

"See, Cassie? You care."

"Of course I care. You were my first love, my only," she said. "I didn't leave because of the way I felt about you."

"Well, you were wrong about the way I felt," he said. "Surely you can admit that now."

"Maybe. I was afraid and I wanted you to see me the same way you had before. Because maybe if you did, I'd still be the same."

Staring at the tips of her loafers, she jumped when he dropped his arm across her shoulders and scooted closer. "Damn that bastard," he said.

"He's pretty damned, all right. Some guy knifed him in jail about eight months ago."

Van went as still as the frozen bench. "Why didn't you tell me he was dead?"

"It wasn't your business anymore."

"Because of your decisions, not mine, and we just talked about him the other day."

"I always thought I'd feel safe if he wasn't around. But I don't. He can't hurt me again, but there are others like him. I want to be big and bad and strong, but something horrible happened to me once, so I can't stop believing horrible things can happen." Dizzy because she'd never admitted she was still afraid, she eased into the heaviness of his arm. "Not that any of this matters now."

"Stay for six months." He turned his head. His breath warmed her temple. She wished he'd kiss her again, and she was surprised. Desire had grown foreign to her. Could she feel it like any other woman?

"What about Hope?"

"I won't pretend," he said. "You know I care about her. I'm learning to care more. I can't help myself, but I'm no saint. Give us six months to see if I can be her father."

"And my—what?"

"Your husband, you idiot."

"You're asking me to marry you?" She half rose, but he pulled her back down.

"You don't have to run for your life. I'm asking you to see if you can love me again."

"Do you love me, Van?"

CHAPTER TEN

"Do I LOVE YOU?" Cold seeped through his bones. His options made him repeat what she'd asked and then kept him silent. Say yes and terrify her so much she panicked all the way back to Washington, or tell her the truth?

"My idea of love has changed," he finally said, blinking a snowflake out of his eye. "It was simple before. You and I, alone. Jobs we both loved. Living together was fun."

"Until I was raped."

Each word stabbed him. He reached for her pink-covered hand and stood, urging her to come with him. "You must be freezing."

"You change the subject every time I talk about what happened."

He faced her. Around them, life went on. A mother called "Tony" in a voice only a mother used. A Salvation Army soldier rang his bell in a sonorous beat. The lights flickered on and off, painting Cassie's skin with a pallor.

"Do you need to tell me?" He'd never forget the first time she'd forced him to listen.

"I need to know you don't hate me for it. You run every time I try to be who I am now."

"I don't want him to hurt you. I want to kill him."

"Too late." She turned toward the street, and her glove came off in his fingers.

He was tempted to let her go. "Why can't we do this my way for once?"

She glanced over her shoulder. She might have been any woman—young, happy, swinging along with commercial-bright independence. "You mean pretending we're the same?"

"I told you I'm not. What are you going to do?"

"Take care of my father. Make sure Hope is as happy as I can keep her, and go home to my job. I haven't even called my partners."

He caught up. "What will they do if you can't go back?"

"I will go."

"Hope told me about a bad guy who came there one night."

She smiled. "I'm glad she can talk about it, but I wish she'd talked to me. It's no big deal. Some guy broke in the night before I left. In fact, I should have called to see what's happening with him."

Fear ran in a trickle of sweat down his spine. Her casual tone didn't help. "Some guy broke in?"

His terror must have seeped into his voice. She

lifted her chin, and he saw only reassurance. "I stopped him."

"How?"

"With the fabled element of surprise and some skills from a good martial arts class that gave me a reason to crawl out of my apartment every day when I first moved to Tecumseh." It was obviously the opening she'd been waiting for. "I take care of Hope and me."

"I know."

"So this talk of us staying comes too late."

And she walked on without him, obviously not even considering his offer to go back with her.

EVERYTHING CHANGED the next day. Cassie woke early. Or maybe she'd stayed awake all night.

Before light, she gave up and went outside for the paper, her bare feet stinging in the cold snow. She made a pot of tea and carried it and the paper to her father's office, where she shut the door and turned on the television to catch the morning news.

She basked in the slow, steady voices of gloom and doom, the inky scent of the paper and her hot tea. It was a luxury to be on her own—absolutely unnecessary to anyone.

Thoughts of Van crept in, but he'd never said he needed her. Just wanted.

The low tug of desire grabbed her. She pressed

her hand to her stomach, her heart pounding as his kiss, his touch, replayed in her mind—and the feelings, so rare in the past five years, spread through her body.

Did she need him?

Questions too disturbing for a rare morning of freedom. She buried herself in the paper again and was startled to find it was past seven when she looked up.

No one stirred upstairs. Her father and Hope must still be asleep. Maybe they'd like a big breakfast. She opened the door to the hall—and found the front door standing open.

"Dad?"

Only the hall's icy cold answered her.

"Dad?"

She ran. He wasn't out front. The street.

Her heart thudded in her ears, shook her whole chest. Cars and snow stood beneath the spiny arms of frozen trees, but there was no sign of her father.

"Oh, my God." She flew back to the front door, sliding across a patch of ice on the wooden stoop. Inside, she bolted up the stairs only to find Hope's door open, too. And her bed empty.

Tears burned her eyes.

How the hell could they have gotten out without her hearing? The TV. But she'd kept it low so as not to disturb them.

What mattered was that they were gone. She stepped into flip-flops and grabbed her rental's keys. She hadn't noticed whether her father's car was in the driveway. She grabbed the banister and skipped most of the stairs getting back down, praying her father's car would be gone. At least if he was driving, he and Hope would be warm.

It sat, encased in ice.

Her cell phone lay on the hall table. She scooped it, ran to the rental, turned on the engine and grabbed the scraper to slash at the snow and ice on the windshield.

Meanwhile, she dialed the sheriff's office. But then she hit the End button.

They'd think she couldn't care for him or for Hope. She'd call them if she reached the main road and didn't find her father and her baby, her innocent, possibly frostbitten baby girl.

She had to call.

She dialed the sheriff again and reported everything. They took her info and promised to send a car. With enough open space on the windshield and windows to drive, she jumped into the car and pulled away from the curb.

Hardly able to feel her frozen fingers, she dialed Van's cell number. It hadn't changed in five years. He answered, sounding sleepy. "Cassie, is that you?"

"Dad and Hope are missing."

"What?" Gone was the sleepy throatiness.

She explained again. "Someone from Tom's office is on his way, but Van, please could you come, too?"

"I'm on my way. Are you waiting at the house?"

"I'm driving toward the road." The lake, its surface half-iced, drew her. "Tell me she wouldn't go toward the water." What kid could resist a layer of ice on a huge expanse of water?

"Leo wouldn't let her. He's forgetful, not insane."

"He's outside in the snow with my baby."

"I'm at my car."

She rounded a car and there was her dad, strolling toward her, his robe flapping over blue polka-dot pajamas, a paper tucked beneath his elbow. Clinging to his hand, Hope skipped in her coat and a knit cap and her blue ski boots.

"I see them," she said into the phone.

"In the water?" Van asked.

"No, no." She hastened to reassure him. "They're walking. Dad's half-naked, but Hope's all bundled up. Will you call the sheriff's office back?"

"Yeah, but I'm still on my way to you."

Cassie stopped the car in front of them and jumped out. "Dad?"

"Uh-oh. Mommy's mad."

With a peek at his granddaughter, Cassie's dad faced her like a chastised teenager. "My paper's gone. I took Mr. Davidson's, but I left him a dollar."

"We're almost a mile from home." She peered over his shoulder, surprised Mr. Davidson wasn't loping after him with a shotgun.

Hope ran into Cassie's arms and she hugged her daughter tight, reassuring herself that her little girl had come through her walk with Grampa unscathed.

"Dad, why aren't you dressed for this weather? You must be freezing."

"I just went to get the paper and then I planned to go right back inside."

She took a deep breath. "What about Hope?"

"I made her put her coat and hat and boots on."

She gave up. "We'll talk at home." She ushered them into the backseat and draped him in the coat she'd left back there the night they'd flown in.

"Someone took my paper without paying. I was going to walk to the market, but a cop told me to go home."

Cassie didn't need Hope's gasp to tell her he was lying. "A cop? No one else is on the street now and no one from Tom's office would have let you and Hope walk down the street with you in your pj's." She ducked back into the car. "We have to return Mr. Davidson's paper."

"I paid for it."

"He wasn't selling it."

"Whatever you want, Cassie. You know best." He started to unfold it, but she leaned into the back and covered the edges with her hands.

"Dad, your paper is at home. I brought it in this morning."

"I only like fresh ones."

Mystified, she eased the newspaper out of his hands. "Then we'll go get you a fresh one."

"I wouldn't go like that." He pointed at her sweatpants and tank top. "The cops like a body to be dressed."

"Still going with that cop story?" She drove as far as Mr. Davidson's and took the paper up to his stoop. Then she ran back to the car to find her father and her daughter laughing as if they'd planned this whole fiasco. If her father were a child, she'd think twice before she'd let Hope play with him again.

She drove to a gas station that also sold newspapers, groceries and "sundries." Before she went in, she tried to tidy her hair and pinched her pale cheeks in the rearview mirror. Finally, she gave up with a disgusted wave of her hand.

Her dad and Hope stopped talking when she came back to the car. Her frustration blossomed into the heartburn of too much coffee on an empty stomach.

"Dad, are you still cold?"

"I feel fine. We think Van drove by while you were in the store."

"He was worried about you so he said he was coming over."

He swapped a look with Hope. Cassie might have been glad they were getting along so well if she didn't seem to be the butt of a private joke between them.

"I've never been so happy to see our house," she said.

"There's Van's car. Oh," Leo said, "he's waiting on the porch."

"I'm hungry." Hope whined for the first time in all their recent adventures. "Grampa can make me cereal."

"I'll make you both breakfast."

"I'm very good at pouring, and I'll watch the news on television. You can have a few minutes with Van."

"Please don't do that."

"I don't know what you're talking about."

"You do, and what you're trying to accomplish is a lost cause." She was lying even as she tried to convince her father. The mere sight of Van made her all breathless.

He came down the steps to meet them as she helped Hope out of her seat, and her father climbed out of the other side of the car.

"Are you all okay?" Van asked.

"I was getting a paper. You two don't have to act as if I was on my way to take out the bank."

"I hope you would have dressed a little more warmly if that was your plan," Van said.

"You've been talking to Cass, haven't you? I don't need parents."

He brushed past Van and went inside the house Cassie had forgotten to lock.

She stared at the open door.

Van picked up Hope. "What came over you, little one? Felt in need of a stroll?"

"That doctor guy told Grampa—Mommy?"

Cassie broke her gaze from the door. "Huh, baby?"

"Is something wrong with the house?"

"I left the door open. I didn't remember to lock it."

Van moved until their arms touched. "I looked it over when I got here. Everything was fine."

"And so are we." Cassie touched Hope's cheek. "What were you saying about Grampa?"

"That man told him not to go anywhere. I couldn't let him leave alone."

"Baby, you're not old enough to be responsible for Grampa."

"Huh?"

"From now on, call me if Grampa wants to go somewhere."

"Okay. Can I eat now?"

"Let's go see what we have. Van, are you hungry?"

"You're asking me to stay?"

"I'm full of surprises today," she said, thinking of the door she hadn't bolted shut. She sighed as Hope hurtled down the hall toward the kitchen. At that age, life was all about the next meal. "Besides, I need to ask someone what kind of preschools Honesty has these days. Which one did your nephew go to?"

"You're staying?"

"I have to call my partners and arrange for a leave of absence, but I can't keep clinging to the hope he'll be able to live on here without us."

"Well, I'm not sure where Eli went. I'll ask Beth which one she'd suggest."

"Thanks." She tried to look him in the eye, but she was too aware that she'd be seeing him often unless she told him once and for all to stay away.

"I should go with you when you enroll her."

She disagreed. They were close to the kitchen, but Hope and Cassie's father were deep in conversation while the TV voices rose, slightly higher than theirs. No one would hear. Now was the moment to send Van away. "People will think you're her father."

"Absolutely, and if I don't go, they'll think someone else was."

She nodded. "That was hard enough to swallow when you did it for my father, but I can't let you imply you allowed me to take your daughter from you—for the whole town."

"Sorry, Cass, but they'll blame you more than me. I don't plan to say anything, just to look as if I belong there."

"To keep anyone from guessing."

"It's still a small town. People will guess plenty. Doesn't mean they'll get anything right."

"They'll talk about you, too, Van."

"I can take it." He tugged at a strand of hair bent at a crazy angle from her face and she remembered she was wearing no makeup, hadn't touched her hair with a comb and was still wearing sleep clothes and flip-flops.

She pushed his hand away, but not before she gave it a quick squeeze whose meaning even she didn't understand. "Come eat breakfast with us."

"MR. VAN, DO YOU HAVE any children in this school?"

They were half inside the L'il Kids building. Thankfully, the woman carrying a stack of paper down the hall hadn't heard Hope's question. "No kids," he said.

"You don't?"

"I'm not even married."

"Neither is my mommy."

That tossed a silent bomb into the conversation. Cassie's face flushed pink. She could use a little more of that color. The past few days had clearly exhausted her.

But why hadn't she ever told Hope she'd been married?

Maybe it hadn't come up with a four-year-old.

Van was relegated to the back wall of the director's office, and then another back wall in Hope's prospective classroom. Hope had been to "school" before so she approached the centers and tables like an old pro.

She even waved a yellow plastic cup crammed full of markers in his direction, like a hunter of old, brandishing her favorite trophy. He felt the teacher watching him.

Funny thing—he liked that they assumed he might be Hope's dad. He tried to believe he only wanted to keep her from being picked on. Who wouldn't go out of his way to protect a child from being told her father was a rapist? Time enough for her to deal with it when she was old enough to understand the labels.

"Do you want to finish the day with us, Hope?" Ms. Amy asked.

Hope started into the air on an excited jump, but Cassie caught her shoulders. "We don't have her things yet. I'll bring her back tomorrow."

"Sounds good. Don't worry, Mrs. Warne. Hope will be happy with us, and I always call right away with any problems—including a difficulty settling in. Welcome to Honesty." She patted Hope's head. "I'm so glad you're joining us."

"Cassie," she said, not bothering to explain further. "Thanks, Ms. Amy. I'm not sure how long we're staying, although I assume we'll be here until the end of the school year."

Hope kept up a prattle about crayons and the "pretty aprons" the children wore for art classes, and learning to play the violin, an extra class the little school offered.

Van kept his silence, and Cassie obviously had plenty on her mind, too. Back at the Warne house, he opened the car door for Hope. Cassie leaned in from the other side to urge her across.

"We'd better get inside and check on my father," she said.

"Want to celebrate Hope's new school with dinner out tonight?" Van put his all into sounding as if it didn't matter.

When Cassie shook her head, disappointment formed a big lump in his chest.

"I have to get some things for Hope and then I need to call Washington. I'm not even sure Dad's up to eating out yet."

He nodded. "Some other time."

Cassie seemed to hear his letdown. She turned Hope toward the small blue house. "Run and tell Grampa about your school. I'll be right in."

"Okay. See ya, Mr. Van."

She ran, all legs and dark hair falling down her back. Van narrowed his eyes, dismayed at the softening of his heart. He was getting too attached to Cassie's little girl.

Cassie shut the other door and came around the car. "I'm not just using you. I'm grateful for what you did today, but I have so much to do. We're going to have to fly home and get some things so we can stay here for a few months."

He noticed "home" was Tecumsch, not Honesty.

"No problem." He climbed back into the driver's seat. "I've been neglecting my own work. See you around, Cassie."

He started the engine but couldn't just leave her that way, watching him with a look he didn't know, from the middle of the street.

He put down his window and leaned out. "Promise you'll call if anything goes wrong—if you need help with Leo."

She nodded, saying nothing. He forced himself to drive away, unaccustomed to sadness lingering like a nimbus around Cassie.

IN THE GATE AREA at Reagan National that night, Van's cell phone vibrated on his belt. He read the number and hit the Talk button. "What's wrong?"

"Nothing." Cassie's laugh sounded brittle

enough to shatter. "I've been thinking of you all day."

His pulse rocketed into double time. "What?"

"Not like that." She was handy with a bludgeon. "I think you left with the wrong idea. It wasn't that I didn't want to have dinner with you, and you know Hope thinks you and 'Grampa' are godlike."

"Does she?" How did Hope's mother feel about that?

"I guess she's missed having men in her life."

"I'm waiting for a flight, and I think they're starting to board."

"Oh. You're leaving town?"

"Business." He'd called a client who always appreciated a face-to-face on his Palm Springs golf course.

"Sorry. I didn't mean to hold you up."

She sounded as if he'd slapped her, and he didn't want that, either. "I'll call you when I get back. Cass—call me if something comes up with Leo while I'm gone."

"What could you do from wherever you're going?"

"Palm Springs, and I'd come home."

"We're not your problem."

"I'm getting that idea."

CHAPTER ELEVEN

"WHY DO WE FIND ourselves in flannel shirts, casting ten-foot fishing lines and throwing candy while Eli gets to ride with his mom in a '67 Caddy?" The parade float, a fishing boat on a papier-mâché lake, jerked forward. Snow stung Van's face as he tossed another handful of candy marked with Beth's lodge's logo into the crowd. "No one who lives here will stay at the lodge, anyway."

"Yeah, but she figures the Christmas parade draws in people from the surrounding counties, and Eli refused to fish." Van's brother-in-law, Aidan, lobbed some chocolate Santas and hard sugar ribbons at the onlookers on the square. "Besides, we're secure enough in our virility that we don't mind small children and teenage girls laughing at us."

"I wish I'd taken your idiot wife up on that fake beard. My face is freezing."

Aidan had grown his own for the past week, in his home office overlooking the real lake. "Too bad clients are put off by a guy who looks like he's been on a bender, huh? How'd the trip go?"

"Fine." Its real purpose had failed. He still thought about Cassie every half hour or so, but at least he hadn't called her. "We celebrated the night Hank's portfolio rose by more than my net worth."

"The stock market's been kind to all of us the past few weeks." Aidan turned and hit Van with a Santa he'd meant to throw at the kids on the street. "You went to one of Hank Bloodworth's parties? I thought you and Cassie—"

"Cassie and I are nothing." Van handed the Santa back. "And a man can go to a party without partaking of all the canapés."

"Yeah? In my experience, Hank doesn't like when you refuse one of his treats." Aidan laughed. "You're an iron man."

Just not interested in anyone except Cassie. He'd been asleep for five years, and that was already too long to wait.

"Mr. Van," a voice that owned his heart shouted. "Mr. Van?"

He saw her on Cassie's shoulders, holding Leo's hand, about ten feet in front of the float. He didn't let himself look at Cassie, though he was hungry for the mere sight of her face. Instead he dug a handful of candy from the barrel and over-handed it Hope's way.

Cassie caught most of it. He cast his fishing line toward Hope, and her giggle made him feel better. Leo waved an *okay* sign, curling his index finger against his thumb.

Beth, far too interested, had to slam on the brakes when the float in front of her stopped, and Van and Aidan had to grab the front of their boat to keep from toppling into the crowd.

"Next year, we get harnesses," Aidan said, "and we don't set foot on this thing until my wife shows us her graduation certificate from a driving school."

"I THINK SOMEONE'S MAD at you," Cassie's father said as they skated behind Hope on the ice rink after the parade. "He waved at me and Hope, and he gave her more than her fair share of treats, but he didn't even look at you. Pointedly."

"Hope, not backwards," Cassie called. "Van's not my husband anymore. He's allowed to like you and Hope, but not me."

"You care about him. You're too stubborn to say so. He's not stubborn."

"He's still my friend. I'd have been lost without him since I came home, but I only need friends these days."

"These years, you mean," her father said in a return to clarity as unwelcome as it was unexpected. "You let that criminal take your marriage away from you."

"Dad, you and I will never discuss what happened without more anger between us than we can stand. Hope, don't skate backwards."

"I'm good, Mommy."

"You need more practice." She thought again. "But not now."

"I'm sorry," Leo said. "I was ashamed back then and I don't know why, but I didn't know how to change my feelings. I didn't want the entire town thinking of you at that bastard's mercy."

"I was at your mercy. I needed you to love me, anyway. I felt at fault because I forgot to shut the window." And yet she'd forgotten to lock the door the day her father had gone wandering, and nothing bad had happened. Life could surprise a woman that way sometimes.

"You were never at fault. I treated you unforgivably, and I didn't know how to make up for it. I couldn't even face myself after you left."

She looked straight at him, maybe for the first time since she'd been home. She could see her father in his eyes. "Is that why you got sick?"

"Maybe." He skated ahead. "Hope, honey, listen to your mom. You're going to fall on your butt."

Hope stopped so suddenly, Cassie ran into her. They both swirled in a circle, as Cassie fought to keep them upright.

"Grampa said butt." Hope could hardly believe it. "Mommy, Grampa said butt."

"Grampa's a grown man. He can choose to say words little girls shouldn't. When you're older, you can say ugly words, too."

"Butt, Cass? You don't think that's one bad word too far?"

"You wouldn't believe how kids her age use it. With face and head and colors and—well, it's best if we just go with it as an avoidable word."

"Sorry, Hope." He parted them. "Shall we continue, ladies? Hope, I remember skating here with your grandmother and your mom."

"What was my grandma like?"

"A queen. As beautiful and regal as a real queen. I don't know why she ever looked at me. And then one day she married me and we had your mommy."

"Lo-o-ove," Hope pronounced it with three syllables. "Jeff McClaren loves me."

Cassie nearly fell through the ice. "Who's Jeff McClaren?"

"A little kid," her father said, and tugged her back to give Hope more room. "Who probably won't be planting a ladder against her window."

His joke distracted Cassie from the pint-sized philanderer with his eye on her daughter. "You're feeling better," she observed.

He nodded. "But that doesn't mean you have to leave me." His plaintive tone was unfamiliar.

"I'll stay until I'm sure you're okay."

"Why don't you want to live here? We're family. Van is your family."

"Van is my ex-husband." She glanced at Hope and then said a grateful prayer of thanks that she didn't turn around and demand to know what an ex-husband might be. "But *you* are my family, and you can count on me and Hope."

"Until you think I'm well enough to get on by myself."

"Not because I don't want to live around you. I'm not sure this is a good place to raise Hope," she said.

"Shouldn't Van have some say?" He lowered his voice. "As much as you?"

Cassie wriggled inside, uncomfortable with the lie her father believed. She disliked lying. For one thing, the truth always showed up, no matter how you tried to discourage it. But this truth might drive her father all the way back to the depths of his illness.

"Van understands," she said.

"No man would, and Van is a family man."

"Mommy, my hands are cold." Hope skated back to them in a wobbling circle.

"Let's get some cocoa to warm them up." She hugged her daughter close. "And you can tell me about this Jeff guy. A Casanova, you say?"

"*Casa* means home in Spanish. I'm learning in my brand-new school." Hope giggled. "You're funny, Mommy. Jeff isn't a house."

"Grampa, are you up for cocoa?"

"Mmm. I love it."

He grabbed Hope's hand and off they skated, together. Anyone else would think him a patriarch, showing off the third generation. But Cassie had seen the dullness come back to his eyes. Just that quickly, he was more Hope's buddy than Cassie's father.

A FEW DAYS LATER, there was another parade, this one with candles and carols.

"You don't think Hope's too young?" Cassie asked her father as they packed a thermos of hot chocolate in her bag.

"We'll bring her home if she doesn't like it," he said. "Come on. I want to go."

Just then the doorbell rang. Leo made for it. "Who could this be? We're not letting anyone hold us up."

While he answered the door, Cassie leaned into the kitchen stairwell. "Hope? Are you ready?"

"Yeah, but I wanted to wear my skirt."

"Your legs would have frozen. Put on the clothes I gave you."

Hope stomped down the stairs in cords and a pale green sweatshirt, her ponytail half-undone on one side and skewed to a spot just over her ear.

"Better let me fix your hair."

"We're gonna be late 'cause you keep fixing me."

"We'll catch up with everyone wherever they are when we arrive," Van said behind them. "As long as we find parking. Everyone gets there at different times."

Cassie turned, the ponytail band in her hands. "What are you doing here?"

Van veered toward her father, who busied himself with a tea towel. "Leo? What happened to Cassie asking me to drive you?"

"Dad?"

"I thought he'd have more room in that big car for us all. We're wearing coats, you know."

"Grampa, you're in trouble again," Hope said as he scurried up the back stairs. Hope took too much joy in her grandfather's machinations. "But I like Mr. Van's car. Who's the present for, Mr. Van?"

Cassie hadn't noticed the lumpy package. He asked her with a look if he could hand it over. She couldn't turn down something for Hope.

"Couldn't get Beth to wrap that for you?" she asked under her breath.

"That's not nice," he said.

"Sorry." She swept a hand toward Hope. "Be my guest."

"It's for me? Oh, boy. Up, Mommy."

Cassie hoisted her onto a stool by the island. "You're getting bigger, my girl."

"I can't get smaller." She folded her hands in her lap, all demure as Van handed her his gift.

"I wasn't sure I'd see you again before Christmas."

She opened the package with uncharacteristic deliberation, plucking the bow off first and then gently peeling the tape back from the paper. But when she unfolded the paper, a white, fluffy stuffed cat tumbled to the floor, followed by a massive box of crayons and a beautiful journal bound in pink leather, printed with white kittens jumping for a ball of yarn.

"Mr. Van." She slid down and scooped up the cat and hugged it so tight her mouth stretched with the effort.

"Hey," he said, his voice thick, "don't I get one of those?"

Tears started in Cassie's eyes even before she saw them welling in Van's. He lifted her girl high and the two of them hugged as if they'd been best friends from the day of her birth.

If only.

The words whispered in Cassie's head, a temptation and an accusation all at once.

She couldn't have stayed. Van hadn't wanted her. The attack had made her stop trusting marriage. She'd known she was carrying a child who'd need unconditional love.

But that part seemed to be coming ridiculously easy to Van.

"Look, Mommy."

Van set Hope down and she brought her haul to Cassie, who knelt beside her. "Wow." She flipped through the journal. "It's perfect for writing your alphabet and for drawing."

"Just like a big girl's."

Cassie couldn't help smiling over Hope's head at Van, whose jaw seemed locked tight. He managed a grin, but then went to the window beside the door.

"Mommy, can I take Kitty caroling with us?"

"Sure. Will you run up and get Grampa? You can show him Kitty."

Hope bolted up the stairs, her kitty's tail flapping beneath her elbow.

With his eyes on Hope's ascending back, Van moved in front of Cassie. "I really didn't know your father was matchmaking," he said.

"I'm not complaining." For the first time in five years, she put her hand on his. "I sent her after him because I wanted to thank you for thinking of my daughter. She's not used to a lot of gifts. Our money's stretched, and sometimes I can't give her things like that beautiful kitty. It's so soft I know it was expensive."

His smile seemed to grow from inside him. Again, he looked away. "Thanks, Cass. That was the nicest thing you could have said."

"But you should be careful about my dad. He thinks you're Hope's father, and he might say so in front of people. He thinks I'm doing you wrong—not giving you enough say in my decisions about her."

He brushed his hand against her sleeve. "I may have made more trouble for you with my quick-thinking but not very well thought out solution."

"I'm thinking of the trouble for you."

"I don't care what anyone says." He leveled his gaze on her. "I never did."

"Cool cat, Van," Cassie's father said as he negotiated the stairs, hand in hand with Hope. "You're going with us to sing carols?"

"Dad, you know Van already gave you away." She laughed at Van's tensed stance. "Accidentally."

"He used to be faster on his feet." At the bottom of the stairs, he tried to lift Hope, but Cassie stopped him.

"You need to get a little stronger, and she likes to walk with you."

"You hold my hand so I won't get lost," Hope said, but she glanced at Cassie as if to say she'd be the one keeping an eye out.

Cassie watched them head for the door, bemused. What a family. All looking out for each other, all sure they knew what was best.

"They'll leave without us, Cass." Van hurried her. "I wouldn't put it past Hope to jump behind the wheel."

"Me, neither, with Dad instigating."

VAN SEARCHED for a quiet moment to caution Leo about trying to set him up with Cassie. She was reluctant enough without her father's overly wholehearted approval.

All night, through countless days of Christmas and about a thousand first Noels, Leo hovered just out of Van's reach, hand in hand with Hope. And always, when Van least expected it, Cassie drifted back to him.

As they sang, she leaned against his arm or smiled into his eyes the way she used to, as if they had a secret that excluded the rest of the world.

Surprise became a slow ache. He knew this woman who still felt like his wife too well. Five years ago this would have been a night for locking the doors and turning off the phone.

They'd have climbed the stairs to their room, still half-furnished because they were waiting to move into their real house, and he traveled so much and she worked just as hard. They'd have switched off the lights and opened the drapes, and the sun would have set on their lovemaking. The moon would have risen on their bodies, twining with devotion only to each other.

But Hope reminded him of the five years that separated the love he craved from the life he could expect. After valiantly keeping up all night, Hope decided she could no longer walk and sing at the same time. She searched for her mom, who'd stopped to speak to her former high school English teacher. Van started toward her.

Hope dragged her hand out of Leo's. She was hand-over-handing up the front of Van's coat when Jonathan Barr approached, wearing a smirk totally out of context with the song of "Good King Wenceslas."

An "Ah, at last I see the truth about you and Cassie" smirk.

Van's first instinct was to set Hope safely out of range and deck the guy. He searched for Cassie among the crowd now cheerfully singing for the medical staff hanging out of windows at Honesty General.

She'd already seen him—and apparently Barr, as well. She sidled between the other carolers, shaking her head until she got between him and Barr.

"No," she said.

"No what, Mommy?"

"Nothing, baby. You like hanging out with Mr. Van?"

"Why don't you go to your mom for a second? I see someone I have to talk to."

"You don't." Cassie put her hands behind her back. "You think you have no choice, and if you didn't—well—I'd be sorry."

He didn't realize he was trying to dance around her until she cut off his access to Barr, who was now laughing. Idiot. How he'd kept his job in the bank was a mystery to Van. He'd never become president, but he must have something on every member of the board to stay employed, considering he lacked compassion or simple human decency.

"Van, no one's in danger. He thinks he's solved a riddle. What do we care?"

"I still need to shove his teeth down his throat."

"Bad man?" Hope twisted to see who they were talking about. "Like that man at home, Mommy?"

"Just a not-very-nice man." Cassie begged him with her eyes to stop.

"I forgot you knocked someone down," he said.

"I thought I had to."

"Then you understand." But he'd lost the will to fight. "I still don't get what you were doing, taking on a man." That wasn't his Cassie, and he'd been too shocked when he first heard the story to demand an explanation.

"He busted into the shelter with a big metal tube. I thought he might kill someone, and..." Her gaze drifted to Hope. "Other people were there. I had to do something, but I feel sick when I think about it. I took classes after we moved to Tecumseh. But how could I think violence was a good choice?"

Hope reached for him and when he took her, she dropped her head onto his shoulder.

"No one needs violence here." Cassie watched Barr fade into the crowd. "I gave my daughter the idea that fighting was all right."

"Fighting *back* sometimes has to be," he said, and then wished he hadn't as she glanced at Hope with worry in her eyes. "Don't be afraid of what'll happen if you stay here."

Her intense expression showed he was right. Hope might have plenty to fight about if the parents of Honesty's toddlers didn't watch their tongues. She shook her head and focused on her little girl's limp body in his arms. "You look tired to me, Hope."

"No." She yawned as wide as the Grand Canyon to prove it

"Let's find Grampa. Where do you think he rambled off to?"

"I've been watching," Van said, only just aware he'd kept Leo's longish gray hair and blue wool overcoat in sight. "He's by the pizzeria sign."

"Don't go far." After a few minutes, Cassie brought her father back and they wove through laughing groups of impromptu singers to Van's car.

"This was fun," Leo said, as Cassie helped Hope with her seat. "Like old times."

"Dad." On automatic, she resisted her father's ongoing matchmaking.

"I'm not saying I wish we could have the old

times again." He turned up his collar and burrowed in. "You remember how awful they were."

As if bidden by Leo's teasing sarcasm, a memory of another Christmas appeared in Van's head. His and Cassie's first kiss, almost an accident beneath the mistletoe in her front hall. He'd touched his lips to hers and started to raise his head, but she'd cupped his nape, drawing him closer, changing forever from a friend into the woman he loved.

It had been that simple.

Then.

"Van?"

She'd turned up in the passenger seat beside him. He stared at her, still half in the past. Her mouth curved, and he remembered the taste of her.

"Van," she said, a note of warning in her voice. She glanced at her father and Hope, clearly to see if they'd noticed the undercurrents in the front seat.

"Sorry." He checked the traffic and pulled onto Square Court. Slowly, they inched around to the road that led to the lake and Leo's house.

By the time he pulled alongside the curb, he'd reined in his errant heartbeat and schooled his breathing into an even rhythm.

Still, he took a lungful of the frozen air outside. Like some lovesick kid, he marveled at ice sparkling on the bare branches and moonlight dusting the streets and houses in an extra translucent layer of light.

"It looks like Santa's coming," he said as Cassie eased her daughter out of the car.

"She's asleep."

"I'll carry her." Leo reached for her.

Cassie turned her hand over and held her father off, but the gentleness in her touch pulled Van like an invisible cord. "I'd like to let you, but she's a big girl. You still have to get steadier on your own feet first."

"You're brutal, young lady."

"Because Hope and I are staying, and I don't want you to take caring for her for granted."

"You're staying?" Over the top of the car, he stared at her, his eyes full of gratitude. In the lamplight, his eyes glittered. Van felt like a Peeping Tom. Leo tapped the car roof. "I'm so glad, Cass."

She smiled, her effort valiant. "Me, too, Dad." She started up the sidewalk. "You coming in, Van?"

How many times had he fabricated an excuse to come over since she'd arrived back home? "Sure." He let her get most of the way to the porch before he punched the button to lock his doors.

They went inside before him. When Van entered,

Cassie had carried Hope upstairs and Leo was still taking off his coat in the hall. Van helped him.

"I'm tired, man. I'm going up to bed, too. Will you be all right on your own until Cassie comes back down?"

Van hung his and Leo's coats in the closet. "Sure. You're not setting us up again?"

"Nope. Too tired, and besides, they're staying. Did you hear Cassie tell me they're staying?"

"I heard, but Leo, don't read more into it than you should. Ask her how long she's staying before you assume anything."

"Forget it." Leo laughed off Van's caution. "But I'll lay off my subtle effort to get you two back together. Suddenly, we have more time to persuade her she should stay home for good."

He turned and started up the stairs, wobbling as if he might tumble backward any second.

"You should have said you were tired."

"I had work to do." He leaned on the banister for several seconds. "But I am exhausted. And sometimes, I think I'm hanging on by a thread. I'm going to bed now before I do anything that will make Cassie think…"

He finished, but Van couldn't understand what he meant, and stopping him again seemed pointless. Van was still staring at the empty landing when Cassie came to it.

"Where's Dad?"

"He went to bed. Did he seem normal to you?"

She leaned over and lowered her voice to match his tone. "I can't hear you."

He waved her down and met her at the foot of the stairs. "Did he seem okay?"

"I don't know. He's pretty obvious about wanting us back together." She pointed to the living room and they went inside. She shut the door behind them. "Even Hope wants to know if you're my boyfriend."

"After such a good evening together—all of us—that disgusted tone hurts."

She lifted her head, shaking back her hair. He sifted a few strands through his fingertips. She pulled away, rubbing her hands down her arms. "You assume you know what I'm thinking."

"The way you assume I don't feel anything. That's what bothers me." He searched her eyes, but she looked away. "Maybe you don't feel anything," he said.

"You know better."

He could barely hear her. He felt as if he was hallucinating.

"Maybe I wanted you to stay tonight," she said.

CHAPTER TWELVE

IT WAS LIKE falling off the side of a building. With only words, she'd knocked the breath out of him. "I don't want to make any more mistakes. What are you saying, Cass?"

She swung away from him. The room's light seemed to go with her. And all his hope, as well.

"I wonder if we might as well give in."

Standing with her back to him, she hid her expression, but she also avoided seeing the hurt he couldn't hide. He dragged his hands over his face.

"Give in to what?"

"Dad. Obviously, Jonathan Barr. Everyone in this town who assumes you're Hope's father, and that I've come home to you as well as to my dad."

"Give in?" He looked for his coat, and then remembered he'd put it in the closet. Besides, he'd be a fool to walk out without answering her. He turned her around. "You think I want you that way? Because you're tired of fighting your family and the people who've loved you all your life?"

"Jonathan Barr? The man's a gossip who loves

nothing and no one better than a juicy tidbit he can spread to any slob who has to beg him for a loan."

"Yeah—your father would have done the town a favor if he'd fired him, but you're not doing him a favor by taking me on."

A shiver started deep in the core of her. He felt it before it shook her body in his hands. She closed her eyes, but then she opened them again, and she looked like the woman who'd blamed him for not loving her.

"I'm afraid."

"Stop it," he said. "I want to stay angry, because you'd let someone else decide if you and I can be together. You could pretend I matter so little to you."

She came to life. It snapped in her eyes as she curved her hands around his wrists. "I care. What I said about giving in was stupid—because I'm afraid."

"How can you not want me back? Deep down, it's all I've wanted since the day you left."

"Even now, when you know I'm different?"

"I want to know if I can love you still—if we can love each other."

She shook her head, hard, and he saw Hope in the strands of hair twisting around her face. "We were a family tonight, and I wondered if I turned my back on my one true love. Five years too late. You think that's not frightening?"

Her hands held him helpless. Unable to move because he wanted her to let go of his wrists and wrap herself around him.

"Cassie, it's like before. You're scared of the wrong things."

"I'm not the same, and you're looking for the woman who left you."

"Cass."

Even he heard his gut-deep need. "I want you back." Her smile was food to him. Her eyes were a sight of the future, of possibilities and love that had abandoned him.

"No." She let him go and she started to move away.

He reached for her. Just in time, he remembered to be gentle. Her shoulders felt too slender, the muscles taut, not his wife's, yielding with love.

She turned her head to hide from him again.

"Do you want me to leave?"

She didn't answer, and he saw the truth. She wasn't certain.

Keeping one hand on her shoulder, he used the other to ease her hair off her face. He brushed the pads of his thumbs over her cheekbones, sharper than even the last time he'd kissed her.

"You had your chance," he said. "I would have gone." He lowered his mouth to her soft skin.

Her scent hadn't changed, sweetness and spice

and everything he knew that made a woman a woman. He kissed the hollow beneath her cheek, and her intake of breath made him dizzy.

He wasn't alone. She needed him, too.

He pulled her close, laughing as her heartbeat fluttered against his chest. She turned her face up, and he kissed her.

He wanted to destroy her with wanting, let the fire that burned inside him lick through her veins.

Instead, it was like before she left. He couldn't stop remembering.

He was afraid of hurting her. He didn't want to remind her of that other man—that bastard he should have killed.

Van pulled away, swearing, without realizing what Cassie would think. She stared, horror in her eyes.

"I told you," she said. "It's too late. Why don't you go?"

"No. I won't leave, and you're going to hear me." He tugged her into his arms. "I need you the way I always did—so much, I'm afraid of hurting you."

He wrapped his arms around her, wary as he felt the outline of her ribs. She'd never gained back the weight she'd lost after the rape.

He pushed those pictures out of his head and grabbed for the other times, fumbling with the sparkling buttons on her wedding dress, breathing through the fall of her hair as she'd leaned over him in their bed, holding his breath as he'd waited for her satisfaction to mount with his.

With a groan, he speared his fingers through her hair and opened her mouth with his thumb. They kissed, two hungry people who each needed to be in charge. Later—later, she could have her way. Just now, he had to show her he still wanted his own. He still wanted her.

He traced the lines of her face with his mouth, learning her anew. Again and again, he returned to her mouth, until kissing her wasn't enough.

She caught his hands at the hem of her T-shirt.

"Wait." Her breath cut the air around them. "Hope and Dad are upstairs."

"Mmm-hmm." He took her mouth again. "I can't stop. Don't make me stop, Cassie."

"We have to." She brought their hands between them. When his knees threatened to buckle, she let him go and slid her arms around his waist.

"The floor," he said, finding her earlobe, letting his teeth caress her. "We've made love there before, and I remember how to lock the door."

She burrowed into his chest, and he held her up for a moment, but she flattened her palms against his stomach.

"I can hardly breathe, Cassie."

"I don't want to stop, either, but I'm Hope's mom, and she's never seen me with someone."

"I'm not someone. I was your husband."

"You're Mr. Van to her." She pushed her hand into his hair, and her skin clung to moisture.

He wanted her so badly he'd broken into a sweat. Laughing, he pressed his lips to the pulse pounding in her wrist. "You're driving me crazy."

"I like you this way better. You acted as if you could barely stand touching me."

He had to see her eyes. "I'm not a subtle man. You must be blind."

She shuddered. "I wish things were different," she said without looking at him.

"Okay, Cassie." He kissed the top of her head, lingering with his cheek against her hair, but not wanting to push. "I'm going home."

"You have to."

Her relief was almost as forceful as the desire that had choked them both. He looked back at her as he went to the door. Emotion seemed to bend her as she reached for the nearest chair.

He wanted to return, but if he touched her again, how would he leave? "You're not afraid of making love with me, are you?"

"No." Her eyes never shifted from his, and he tried to blame his doubt on the habits of five years.

"MOMMY, IF MR. VAN IS my daddy, why doesn't he live with us?"

If Van was her daddy? She must have heard it

at school. Cassie couldn't say he wasn't, so she backpedaled. She scanned the produce section, but they were nearly alone tonight in the market. Another snow had kept most sensible people indoors. "You know moms and dads sometimes live apart." She put a tomato in the plastic bag Hope was holding out. "We've seen a lot of that at home."

"But those fathers wanted to hurt the mommies and the children. Did Mr. Van hurt you once upon a time?"

She smiled at Hope's idea of the past. It was always "once upon a time" for her. "Never. Mr. Van would never hurt anyone."

"He doesn't love us?"

"I think he loves you. He and I can't live together."

"Nope. I don't unnerstand."

"Me, either, but let's be friends with Mr. Van, and someday, you'll have a daddy like any of your friends."

"Will he live with us?"

"When you have a daddy, he'll live with us." She put another tomato in the bag, and they closed it together, Hope twirling it and then handing it to Cassie to knot.

"Will he love me, Mommy?"

"Baby." Cassie knelt beside her. To the strains of a tinny "White Christmas," she hugged her daughter so tight Hope grunted. "Everyone with any sense at all loves you."

"Okay, but you're squishing me."

"CASSIE, I'VE HEARD about your shelter. I saw you speak at a conference in Maryland two years ago."

"I wish you'd spoken to me." Knowing Allison Blaine, director of the state-run women and children's shelter in her hometown, had been in that audience seemed odd. "I haven't seen that many friends since I left."

"I'm not sure when I last had an actual vacation to visit friends." Something on her computer screen made her jot a note on a small yellow pad. "Must be the same for you. I'm sorry your father's illness had to be the thing that brought you back." She looked up. "Sorry about the e-mail. I'm sure you understand how busy I am."

"That's why I'll cut to the chase. I need a job while I'm here."

A tone rang on the computer, and Allison's attention split to the screen again. "How long do you plan to stay?"

"That's open-ended. I won't pretend this is a permanent change, but I could ease your workload around here."

"We always welcome new volunteers, and I'm in the process of requesting funding for a new position, but I've been budgeting for a full-time, permanent person."

Cassie regarded the serviceable oak desk, clearly a castoff from a schoolteacher's classroom. The filing cabinets, four across, were each a different primary color, obviously hand painted. The building itself creaked with the footsteps of each inhabitant.

Full-time. Permanent.

"I'm not just saying this because I need the job, but I could be here on a permanent, full-time basis." Cassie gripped her chair's arms. "I'm not sure what's happening with my father, but I may not be able to leave."

"And you wouldn't mind being an employee after you ran the shelter in Washington?"

"Even if I did mind, the job matters more than who gives the orders. And I need work."

"My sister told me you're looking for a nurse."

"Jill works for the Caring Heart service?"

"You knew she was a nurse?"

"I remember."

Allison drew a line under her last note and scribbled another. "Would you be able to work full-time hours with your father's needs?"

"Right now he needs someone to check on him at mealtimes to make sure he's eating, maybe once or twice during the workday to make sure he has what he needs. His care will eventually change, but he seems to be improving with us there."

Allison capped her pen and turned the monitor, as if to remove herself from its temptation. "Let's take a look around the place." She shared the wry smile of a colleague. "See if you're still interested after you see the extent of *our* needs."

Cassie's relief was a lump in her throat. It wasn't just the money. She needed to do something worthwhile, and she and her father hadn't lived together in over a decade. They both needed an occasional break. He'd already begun to turn back into his room and pretend he had vital business if she passed him to take laundry to the linen cabinet or stopped to ask if he needed anything

A short tour brought her and Allison back to the other woman's office. "As you can see, we're not as state-of-the-art as you," she said.

"No one is state of any art in this work, but we've done a lot of private fund-raising and we're not bound by state rules."

"You're still interested if we get the position?"

Cassie nodded. If only the rest of her decisions were so clear. "What kind of time frame are you looking at?"

"We're close. I'd say no more than a month."

Cassie picked up her purse and the dark green folder in which she'd carried her résumé. "That sounds good. I'm still settling my dad." She rubbed her temple. "Although he'd say he was settling me."

"My parents are the same, and they're hale and hearty." Allison extended her hand. "I'm glad you came in. We need your experience. I was looking at extensive training for whomever we hired, so maybe I'll be able to work a little more into your salary. You know, Cassie, if you needed to bring your father into the center every so often, that wouldn't be a problem. We could use the influence of a good man. The children we see haven't been exposed to someone like Leo Warne."

"Thanks, Allison. I needed to hear that. He's different."

"Losing a parent, even over time, is terrifying. Who wants to be your father's parent?"

"And what father wants to admit that's happening?"

They shook hands, a commiserating smile giving Cassie the feeling they'd bonded. Since she'd returned, she'd known sharp, infrequent moments when she felt she'd come home. It was a peculiar side effect to interviewing for a job.

"Have you seen much of Van?" Allison asked.

Two nights ago came back like a memory that wanted to be relived.

"You're not afraid of making love with me, are you?" he'd asked.

"My father still considers him family," Cassie said, unable to find any other answer.

"We're that kind of a town. No chance to put an ex-spouse behind you." Allison led her into the hall.

"You don't have to walk me out." She couldn't face any more talk of Van. "I remember the way."

"Good. Then we'll speak when I hear on my funding."

Allison returned to her business day, but she'd destroyed Cassie's brief, false sense of security.

She left the shelter, her arms around her waist, remembering Van's strength. Fear beat again in her throat, unexpected, unwished for.

Making love with him long ago had been as right, as easy, as breathing. She'd longed for him to hold her the old way, heedless of anything except their need for each other. But as desire had replaced the gentleness of his touch, she'd searched the darkness behind her closed eyes for escape.

Van had left her mind, and that other being had taken over. How would she open herself to any man? The rape hadn't been sex, but somehow sex had become dangerous, even when it was an act of intimacy she deeply wanted with Van.

Cassie shook her head.

In the car, she took out her cell phone and called the shelter in Tecumseh. She couldn't count on privacy at home.

Home. The mere word scared her. She was getting worse instead of putting the past behind her.

Kim Fontaine finally picked up the phone on the other end. "Cassie?"

"Hey. I need to talk to you and Liza. My father is ill enough that I need to stay here a while, so I'd like to discuss a leave of absence."

"I hate to hear that. We miss you."

"The extra set of hands, you mean?"

"That, too." Kim laughed. "But we miss you as well. Why don't we schedule a call when Liza can join us, and we'll talk about what comes next. You aren't pulling out?"

Cassie took a deep breath, scanning the bare hardwoods and the gently waving pines that surrounded Honesty's shelter. "Not yet, but it could come to that."

"Man."

"Yeah."

Too restless to work at home, Van had taken his laptop to Grounds Up, a coffee shop just off the square. If you ignored the new age music and the strange Zen names they applied to their brew, it was a great place to take advantage of free WiFi.

Conversation among the other customers forced him to stop thinking of Cassie and pay attention to making his livelihood.

"Refill on your Samsara blend, Mr. Haddon?"

He chose not to ask the girl with the stud in her nose why she wasn't in school. That first cup had powered him through two days of neglected e-mail and the start of a new promo letter. "Sure," he said.

"Two shots?"

"Better not this time."

His erratic heartbeat probably had more to do with memories of Cassie in his arms, her body moving with his, her breath coming in sharp pants that drove him nearly out of his head. But why ruin a perfectly good heart?

The young girl took his cup back to the counter. Stretching after so long at his laptop, he glanced out the plate-glass window. Across the street, a line of children held one another's hands as they made their way around the courthouse's wrought-iron fence. Over their coats, they each wore the pastel pinafores that proclaimed them students of the L'il Kids school.

Van searched the straggling line for Hope. There she was, five from the end, wriggling to free herself of the little boy behind her.

She turned, her face flushed, her hair flying as always with the rush of her emotions. Van frowned. Normally, she was laughing or eager to escape for an adventure.

Halfway to his feet, he saw anger on her face.

Was she crying?

He hit the door at a trot. It slapped open in his hands.

Hope's voice rose above traffic noise and the whistle of the cold pre-Christmas wind that tickled the coffee shop's chimes and the tinsel the town had hung to celebrate the holidays.

"My daddy is not a bad man," Hope shouted.

Van was running. A car honked on his left. He didn't bother to look. Hope was yanking her hand out of the little creep's behind her with all her might.

Jonathan Barr's kid. Not a creep, but a parrot for his father's point of view.

"Mr. Van." She said his name as if he'd swooped like Superman out of the sky to save her.

"What's up?" He fought irrational anger toward the little kid who dropped her hand at last.

"That boy says my daddy is a bad man." She charged him. Van caught her. A teacher from the school had noticed at last.

"Mr. Haddon, may I ask what you're doing?"

"I'm—" He'd started to say Cassie's husband. "A friend of the family's. I saw her crying. May I speak to you?"

"Are you my daddy, Mr. Van?"

The other teacher approached, and her interest rivaled the first woman's. Even the kids seemed intent. He only hesitated because Cassie was the first of his concerns, and she wasn't going to like this.

"Yes," he said. And to hell with Cassie's anger. She'd understand when he told her this kid had hurt her little girl.

Both teachers goggled at him, fish in the small-town bowl they'd all grown up in.

"May I take her home?"

"We'll deal with young Josh," the first woman said, old enough to clearly think she should deal with Van, too. "Hope should stay. This is her class, and she's as important as any of our other students."

"You'll keep an eye on the situation?" Would a real father feel any more reluctant to drop his daughter into a toddler's version of a viper's nest?

"Absolutely." She reached for Hope, who clung to Van. "This is part of life, Mr. Warne."

"She's a little young for life lessons."

"Sadly, not. And you're not authorized to take her home from school. Certainly not in the middle of a field trip."

On the verge of telling the woman to call Cassie, he noticed the other children nudging each other and realized he might make things worse for Hope. He set her on the ground, tugging at her coat and the pinafore that covered it.

"Don't go," she said.

He kissed her forehead and wiped her tears

away. "I'll see you at home tonight." That was for Josh Barr, a reminder that Van was watching and he shouldn't bully a little girl—no matter what his father's habits might be. "Have fun on the rest of the field trip."

"Come up here and walk with me, Hope." The first teacher took her hand. "You can be our line leader."

Immediately brightening at the promise of being in charge, Hope let go of Van and skipped beside the other woman.

Van's anger dissipated with a thump in the region of his chest. He'd overreacted.

Even Josh took the hand of the kid in front of him without holding much of a resentful-eyed grudge.

Cassie. He'd better tell her before the neighbors began to congratulate her on finally bringing his baby home to him. He'd be lucky to survive his latest move.

"CASSIE, LOOK who's here. Van."

Her father's excitement had given her no chance to guess. She looked up from sorting Hope's socks on the living room floor to find her father and Van in the doorway.

"What's up?" She tried to sound as if she didn't care, as if she hadn't spent three days—nights, actually—dreaming she hadn't lost her nerve and sent him away. Three nights of dreaming she'd made love with the tall, lean man who loomed over her, worry creasing lines in the center of his forehead.

"Leo." He rammed his hands into his overcoat pockets. "Can I have a few minutes with Cassie?"

"Take all you want." Her father all but danced. He pointed upward. "I'll be in my room."

"You don't have to—"

"He does, for just a few minutes."

She stood, oblivious to her father's quick exit. "What's the matter?"

"Hope's fine," he said, and that really scared her, "but I saw her with her class on a field trip."

"They're touring the courthouse." As if that mattered. "What happened?"

"The kid behind her was bugging her. She kept trying to get away from him, but they were holding hands the way the kids do on field trips."

"You're terrifying me."

"I told her and everyone in her class, including the teachers, that I'm her father."

She saw it with perfect clarity. Miss Amy and Mrs. Doris, the other children pausing in the communal yelling of "fight" only to gape at Van, claiming to be the new girl's dad.

"Oh, no. I knew she'd heard it there, but I never dreamed you'd say it."

"I think I overreacted, but she was crying. One of the other kids was teasing her."

Cassie stopped minding for a second. She scattered socks on her way to the door. "I'll go get her."

"Now you're overreacting. I'm telling this badly because I'm afraid you'll say you never want to see me again."

"Tell me the right way, then."

"She's fine. The older teacher let her be line leader, and she skipped off, happy as a clam."

Cassie's relief felt like bubbles. "She'd rule the world if people would just get out of her way and let her go about her business."

"But Josh Barr apparently told her either I was her dad or someone she interpreted as a bad man might be."

"I don't want her to think a bad man..." She gathered her wits as the enormity of Van's false confession washed over her. "But now you're her father in the eyes of everyone you know—of people you don't know who just remember I was raped and we got divorced."

"I don't care about that." He brushed it away with a wave of his capable fingers. "I just don't want Hope to be more hurt when she finds out the truth."

"Someone will figure it out. Someday, someone will tell her. Or she'll ask me, and I'll have to tell her."

"When she's old enough to deal with it." He came to her, also kicking balled-up socks. As if she couldn't hear or understand without his hands on her. "I'll be the first to untangle the mess I've made. I'll explain to her, but how does a four-year-old cope with her classmate calling her a rapist's daughter?"

Tears hurt Cassie. She never let herself cry. "That's who she is, Van."

"No." He held her. A compulsive tangle of emotion. She hugged him back, trying for once to comfort him.

"Yes, but I love her, anyway, with all my heart—and I think you're learning to."

"I don't care what he did. He's never been her father." He stepped back, enough to look down at her, with a new need. "I'll be her father."

As if that settled something for him, he dragged Cassie close again, and his mouth took hers with the force she remembered, with affection and need and the conviction of true, lasting love.

She tasted coffee and the texture of Van, wanting her, making love that made her forget the world as his hands drew her into the blessed contours of his beloved body.

She kissed him back, cradling his face, rediscovering her own soul in the wonder of touching him. He covered her hands, as if to keep her from pulling away.

His mouth traced her face, every curve, every angle, and she basked in his unconcealed longing. He kicked the door shut behind him, and they tumbled onto the couch.

"I want to see you." He rolled until she was straddling him, one knee buried in the cushions, his arousal beneath her, pulsing with each beat of his heart.

She stroked his face again, exulting in his excitement, but when he arched into her, her own need ebbed, and the terrifying emptiness cracked open in her heart. A sliver of the pain it used to be.

Van pulled her down. He opened her mouth with his, but it was too late. How could he not notice? He moved against her, kissing her, nudging the sides of her shirt aside with his questing mouth. He undid the top button.

She gasped for air.

He lifted his head, and she felt stubble against the rise of her breast, then his lips, drawing her skin into his mouth, his tongue tasting her.

"No." She drew back so sharply she fell to the floor. "No." She drew up her knees and wrapped her arms around them, defending herself against any touch.

Van's arms and legs relaxed in perfect, heartbreaking surrender.

"No?"

She shook her head. Who knew if he could see her as he lay on his back, staring at the ceiling?

"Because of me or him?"

"I thought I could do it." The words bubbled out of her, a confession she had no intention of making. "You were my husband. I know you, your body. You're—"

"Safe," he said.

"I thought so."

He stood, his legs ungainly, as if he'd suffered a fatal electrical shock.

"I don't want you that way," he said. He staggered to the door. His footsteps went down the hall, and the front door opened and then shut again.

She fell into emptiness like a well. Cassie, who never let herself cry, couldn't stop. She buried her face in the couch that smelled of must and her father's house.

At last, as if she were hovering over her own head, she heard Van's name, over and over, in her sobbing voice. She covered her mouth with both hands to keep anyone else from hearing.

CHAPTER THIRTEEN

LATE THAT NIGHT, she called. He stared at her number on his phone and considered not answering.

They had to face the truth and learn to live without each other. After five years, it was about time.

He clicked the Talk button. "Hey."

"I'm sorry."

"I won't be your fallback position."

"I'm not asking you to, Van. I want you. I want more children and a life."

"But you can't let me touch you. And you can't make yourself touch me. I'm not safe, and you're afraid no one else will be."

"Maybe I need time."

Her voice, drenched in misery, made him want to reach for her through the phone. Even in the old days, admitting weakness hadn't been her strong suit. "I'm trying to say something comforting, but I'm tired, Cassie, and I don't like thinking I've been wrong all along. I thought if we loved each other, it would be enough."

"We never gave each other time."

"You left," he said, "and now that you've come home, we have been together but we found out today that time means as little as love."

"Van—"

"I can't," he said.

"Can't what?"

"Settle. I love you too much to pretend being your safety net would be enough. And since I can't even be that, we might end up hating each other. I couldn't live with that."

"You love me?"

He nodded. Of course, she couldn't see him. It didn't matter. In the darkness of his own empty house, he pulled the phone away from his ear and pressed End.

"I HOUNDED the funding office until they found money for me," Allison said over Cassie's cell phone on Christmas Eve morning. "So, what do you say? You can start the second week in January, after we finish the drug testing and fill out all the forms."

"That'd be great." Cassie was waiting for Hope to come out of her school, but she wanted Allison to know how pleased she was.

Yet something happened when she realized she had to stay now. The wall she'd fought free of, that had separated her from the world and kept her from feeling anything, had emerged straight out of the ground again. "Thanks, Allison."

"Is something wrong? Are you having second thoughts?"

She should change her name to Second Thoughts—or Total Doubt. "Are you kidding? I'm grateful. This job will be such a help to my family."

"You'll be a help to us. Drop by any time you want. I'll call you after the holidays with a test date."

"Thanks."

"We'll be the ones thanking you. I see more time with my own family on the horizon. Your résumé was an unexpected Christmas present."

"You're making me feel welcome. I'm grateful."

"We live in a small town, Cassie, but we have problems like any other place." A silence waited for Cassie to fill it. "I'm sorry," Allison said. "You know as well as any woman who's come to us."

"It's not a problem. I don't mind talking about it."

She'd spoken of it many times, except with Van. She felt guilty when she tried to talk about the rape with Van. "My daughter's preschool is letting out. I'd better go now."

"See you in the new year."

Cassie got out of the car and ran to meet Hope,

who was sporting a Christmas-decorated bag of
goodies. Cassie and Hope had provided cookies
for the class.

"Lookie, Mommy." Hope opened her bag and
showed off candy canes and wrapped chocolates,
a plastic bag of cookies like the ones she'd con-
tributed, and a couple of pencils topped with
Santa and Rudolph erasers.

"What a haul," Cassie said. She rubbed Hope's
hands. "You're freezing. Where are your mittens?"

"I lost them." Hope hurried to the car, climbed
behind the steering wheel and then crawled into
the back and her booster seat. "Gotta show my
stuff to Grampa. He likes cookies."

Cassie checked to make sure she was secure
and then drove home. Leo met them at the door.

"Cookies?" he asked Hope, who was already
holding her bag wide for him to see. "Yummy.
Those look almost as good as the ones you and
your mom made, but I'm glad you got new ones,
'cause yours are almost gone."

"Dad," Cassie said as if she were the parent,
"you're not supposed to eat a dozen cookies at
once."

"I don't think I ate them all."

She didn't argue. His clarity seemed to improve every day. The worst decisions he made
were about diet and he was ultra aware of Hope

when he looked after her, but Cassie was still grateful for the job that would allow her and Hope to stay.

"Let's see what we have to leave Santa tonight. Then Hope and I want to visit Killarney's Department Store. I've heard Santa's there today."

"I need to tell him what I want, Grampa."

"Good idea. Go straight to the source, young lady. And maybe you should bring home some chocolate-covered cherries, Cass. Remember how your mom loved them?"

"Come with us, Dad."

"Let me get dressed."

Hope went to the bathroom and then got a glass of milk while they waited. In a little while, Cassie's father called her from the top of the stairs.

She went to see what he wanted and found him in a dark blue suit with a strange—for him—chartreuse tie whose wrinkled ends he held up.

"I don't know…" He moved the ends up and down again. "I used to be able to—"

"That's okay. I can do it." She ran up the stairs to tie it before he could get upset. "You taught me when I was a little girl."

"Why?"

"I don't know." She shrugged. "I guess I was curious, so I asked you."

"I forget things," he said over her hands. "I don't know why."

"Everybody forgets." She kissed his cheek. He'd remembered to shave. "Don't upset yourself, Dad. I forget stuff all the time."

"Guess that's what happens when you live a busy life. Hey, did you hear anything on the job?"

"See? I forgot to tell you. I got it."

"So you're staying?"

His relief made her want to cry some more, God forbid.

"I'm staying, and Santa's waiting for us. We'd better go." She hugged him, trying to ignore a spurt of anxiety at the thinness of his shoulders.

"Mommy, I have to go to the bathroom again."

THE LINE at Killarney's took forever in Hope's eyes. Surrounded by faux snow and Christmas carols blanded down to elevator music, and surprising knots of late shoppers, she grabbed the spirit of the season by the throat.

Despite Leo and Cassie's best efforts at holding her back, Hope danced and sang and hopped and apologized when the people around them stared.

All the while, Cassie dreaded the moment. Hope had melted down before when faced with Santa in all his Christmas red-and-white abundance. When her turn finally came, she let go of Cassie's hand and peered up at her, a picture of earnestness.

"Will you wait here?"

Cassie rocked on her heels, and the father of two anxious boys behind her sighed with gusto. She ignored him. "Are you sure?"

"I have to ask Santa a secret."

"Oh. Okay. Call me if you need help."

Hope started at a run up the red carpet. Her speed slowed as the green elf took her hand. By the time she reached Santa, she was a bowstring of reluctance.

She tried to climb into his lap, but as he held out his hands, she backed off.

"Maybe you should go," the man behind Cassie said.

"Maybe."

But Hope reached a compromise. She leaned into Santa's leg and he leaned down to hear her request. He immediately stared at Cassie, and she found herself wondering what went on behind Santa's cotton beard and white caterpillar brows.

Santa seemed to find a compromise, too. He said something to Hope. She grabbed him in a hug that practically unmasked him and a flash-bulb went off. With a grin as wide as her face, she danced back to Cassie.

"Time to go, Mommy."

"Little girl?" The elf chased her down, to hand Hope a small burgundy bag and Cassie a photo that was still developing.

"Thanks," Hope said and Cassie echoed her.

The elf patted Hope's shoulder and then took the two boys behind them and went back to work.

"What'd you get?" Leo asked.

She pried the drawstring open. "Ooh, look, a bendy Rudolph. And a teeny coloring book." She shut the bag. "I'm sleepy, Mommy."

Cassie held out her arms, amid a sea of yawning children. "Jump up here and I'll carry you to the car."

Hope was asleep before they got home. Cassie carried her up to bed and changed her into pajamas. Leo tucked her in, bringing a glass of water to leave at her bedside.

"She'll be up early to see what Santa brought," he said. "I'm looking forward to it myself." He hugged Cassie. "For the first time in I don't know when."

"Me, too." She pressed her forehead to his. "Let's go down and plant some cookies and a glass of milk. You hungry?"

"Enough to do the cookie-and-milk ritual."

They set a half-eaten cookie and an empty milk glass on the hearth and then Leo put all the presents under their tree.

"I'm pretty tired," he said. "I might go to bed, too."

"Okay. I'm a little keyed." She eyed snow fluttering past the windows in the darkness. "I might take a walk down to the lake."

"You think? We still have the boathouse. I never dropped the rent on it." He rubbed her back, the way he used to. "Your mom loved that place."

"Yeah."

"Well, don't be long."

"Okay. Night, Dad." She kissed him. "I think Santa may be good to you, too."

"He's already been the best. I have you and Hope and a tree all decorated for once—even if it looks as if it's dying to plunge through the window. How could I ask for more?"

She laughed. "I'm glad you love Hope."

"I wish I'd loved you better, honey."

Her throat tried to shut. She swallowed, hard. "You're doing okay."

With a grin very like Hope's, he started up to bed.

Cassie put her coat back on and grabbed a flashlight from the closet shelf. She eased through the front door, locked it and slipped the keys into her pocket.

At the end of her own driveway, she could see Beth's lodge across the lake. Lit up like a Christmas tree itself, it looked more festive than the house behind her. She glanced back.

She'd been wrong. The tree in the window glowed red and green and orange and white and blue. Not the most fashionable, themed or white-lit tree, but it looked like home. And two of the people she loved were in there behind that glow.

She looked toward Beth's house again. Was Van in there? He probably spent Christmas Eve with his sister and her family.

Times that once she would have shared, too.

She wandered across the road. In the darkness, the terrain had changed over the past few years. She searched among pointy branches and high weeds for the path to the boathouse.

A neighbor on the lake owned most of them, as well as the docks. He rented them and kept them up. Thank goodness, she thought as she stepped onto the dock. If her father had been responsible for upkeep, she might have gone straight through the decking.

It was as sturdy as ever, and Cassie walked out over the lake, blinking snow from her eyelashes. Ice had begun to form, a see-through layer about ten feet away from shore. The air washing over it made her shiver. She went on to the boathouse.

It meant so much to her, this place.

They'd given up the boat a long time ago, right after her mother's death. She tiptoed to look through the window. Deck chairs and cushions lined the slip.

The same cushions? The ones she and Van had used that first time...

It might be Christmas Eve. The night was freezing cold, and snow stung her face, but old memories, filled with the warmth of living, had brought her down here.

She tried the door. It wouldn't open and she tried it again, feeling shut out, remembering Van's arms around her, his voice whispering that they could stop, they didn't have to…

She'd never wanted anything more than making love with him. And she thought maybe, if she could see the place where they'd first loved each other, she'd find the courage to trust him, to share her body with him again.

A combination padlock held the door shut, but a piece of paper in a plastic bag was hooked to the lock's hasp. She took out the paper and unfolded it, holding it beneath her flashlight.

"Leo, I locked the door because we've had some vandalism on the lake. Call me if you want the combination. Van."

"I was trying to stay away like he asked."

She whirled, skidding so that Van hurried to her.

"Are you all right?" he asked.

"You startled me."

"I saw that. You shouldn't be out here in the snow. Your hands are like ice."

"Yours, too."

"Let's go inside."

"Let's go into the boathouse."

He hesitated, confused. "What are you doing out here?"

"Walking. What about you?"

"I was at Beth's. We exchange gifts on Christmas Eve. When I was leaving, I saw your flashlight over here. Some kids have been breaking into the empty boathouses, so I thought I'd check."

"You sound serious." She didn't want to be serious, and she wouldn't mind if he swept her away from everything that frightened her.

"Why are you out here, Cass?"

"I was thinking of you. I feel unsettled. I didn't want to go to bed." Alone. "Take your pick."

He didn't answer, but she could hear him breathing in the darkness.

"He never asked you for the combination?"

"No. This place means your mom to him. He doesn't want to remember. I remember the combination, though. Do you really want to go inside?"

"I don't know." Her nerve evaporated. "It must be dusty. I'll bet all that stuff is rotting."

"No." He moved around her and opened the lock. His body's warmth seemed to envelop her. She kept her distance. "I clean it every so often."

She stopped on the threshold. "Why do you do that?"

"I've asked myself many times." He turned the door handle. "The first time, I saw the door open so I added the padlock and I oiled this. It was almost frozen. As I said, your dad had already asked me to stay away." His grimace implied that meeting had been ugly and mean. "So I left the note."

"I don't understand." She walked inside, only realizing how cold it was when they left the blowing snow outside.

"Maybe seeing me was painful when he couldn't be with you." He shut the door behind them. "I felt that way, too."

"How, Van?"

"How?"

She took a deep breath. "How did you keep feeling that way? I tried to put you behind me."

His smile was a balm, teasing, kind. "Don't think I mooned around for five years, pining for you. I thought I'd moved on." He switched on the lights. Water, licking at the sides of the slip, looked dark green and thick. "But you're everywhere for me in Honesty. Beth said many times I either needed to find you and start over or stop thinking about you and learn to love someone else."

She lifted her hand to the front of her coat. "Funny how much that hurts. I didn't leave because I wanted to make you suffer. There were days when I wished you'd ignored everything I said." She pushed her hair away from her face. "Sometimes when I was alone, staring out my window into the darkness because I needed to make sure no one else was staring back at me, I thought—"

"I hate thinking of you being afraid."

"I thought," she went on as if he hadn't spoken, "that you might come, and if you did, I could believe you really loved me."

He slid his hand between the lapels of his jacket and the snaps popped open, revealing a navy sweater. "Would it have been that easy? If you wanted to test me, why not just tell me what you needed?"

"I didn't know. I was all feelings, and no feeling at all. Eventually, I focused on Hope and told myself keeping her safe was all that mattered."

"We've both been asleep," he said. "Five years of unconsciousness, but you and I were meant for each other. We had no one else to turn to."

"Do you feel that way?" If only she could believe. If only she could close her eyes and... No, he needed her with her eyes wide open.

"Nothing's changed since the other night, Cass. I still don't want you back because you think I'm the only one you'd feel safe with." He flung the door open. "Not that it matters, since you don't even feel safe with me."

Footsteps echoed on the dock outside. Cassie moved to the door. "Hope," she said. "Or Dad."

Sheriff Tom Drake, his hand on the holstered pistol at his side, appeared in the doorway.

Cassie fought an illogical compulsion to laugh. "Hi, Tom."

"What are you two doing here? McCauley,

down the lake, said someone was vandalizing your father's boathouse again."

"We weren't vandalizing." Cassie felt like a teenager, caught making out in a car.

"Do you know it's snowing? Santa's on his way. Go home, the pair of you, and don't drag me out in this weather again."

"We're on our way," Van said. "Sorry, Tom."

"Ah, don't worry about it. I gave my deputies the night off because they all have kids. I'm feeling left out myself. If I had a boathouse, I might go wallow with a little Christmas spirit and mull over the state of my life."

Cassie shot him a sharp look, her mouth open to deny doing anything of the sort, but Sheriff Drake was right.

She'd become a parent to her father.

She'd brought her daughter to a place where adult gossip made her think she needed to kick the crap out of a kid because her mommy had stopped a "bad man" that way. Cassie was going to have to help Hope find a better way to face that challenge during her time in Honesty.

She glanced back at Van—the man she loved, still. Always.

Tom waited for him, and Van waited for Cassie to walk out of the boathouse. She hit the light switch, to keep Van from seeing the truth in her eyes.

Tom's flashlight was more a beacon, no doubt visible from the International Space Station. He lit the way up the slight rise to the road, but Cassie had left her own flashlight in the boathouse, and she climbed in total darkness.

She knew what she had to do. She'd seen a rape counselor and a psychologist for three years, but his training hadn't taken as well as her martial arts instructor's.

Her body had the right instincts. That night at the shelter, she hadn't thought. She'd simply responded to the danger to her and her child and her charges. Her body hadn't needed any input from her mind or her heart.

Her heart, her mind—they'd had equally intense training, but no one could break down the fear that held her immobile, unable to trust.

At the top of the hill, Van turned toward his car. "Night, Tom. Cass, I'll stop by tomorrow to see Leo and Hope, if you don't mind."

Now or never. Take her own battering ram to the doors she'd shut on trusting any man ever again, or just live behind them.

The thing was, there'd been someone to knock down—someone to stop in the attack on the shelter. How did she stop herself?

How could she wake herself from five years of stupor and start living again?

CHAPTER FOURTEEN

SILENCE FILLED his house like a poisonous fog absorbing every molecule of oxygen. He roamed from room to room, lost and alone.

He should have followed Cassie to Washington. He should have planted himself on her doorstep so that she had to tire of stepping over him or invite him in.

Five years later, she could hardly be clearer about being through with him. The worst part was that he hated to think of her alone for the rest of her life.

Who was he kidding? She'd meet someone. She was a good, loving woman, still capable of great happiness, of laughing with her daughter and her father. Somewhere inside, she still had the capacity to love and trust.

She just couldn't find love and trust enough to be with him again.

Just past midnight, he went to bed. A little after one in the morning, he gave up and climbed out of the twisted sheets. Downstairs, he started a blaze in the living room fireplace and made a pot of coffee. Then he sat in front of the TV, watching Santa progress reports and a snooker tournament taped in Liverpool last spring.

When the doorbell rang, he discovered how it felt to jump out of his skin.

His thoughts went to Beth and her family as he hurried to the door. The woman outside, shivering in jeans and a sweater too light for the weather, had once been his wife, but the fear in her eyes made her a stranger.

"Don't send me away, Van."

"Are you nuts? Come to the fire."

He led her, vibrating like the strings of a violin, to the hearth, sat her down and wrapped an afghan around her shoulders.

"What are you doing here? Who's looking after Hope?"

"My dad. He's alert when he's with her, and I left my cell number on his door with a note that he should call me if she woke up."

She huddled into the blanket, her teeth chattering. "This wasn't part of my plan."

"Your plan?"

"I meant to walk in, drag you to the bedroom and show you I can be a wife again."

He stared at her. It wasn't that she'd never dragged him to the bedroom before.

"But the house has changed so much, I stood

out there staring at it and I realized I don't know where the bedroom is."

"Same place it always was. I wish you'd been here that night. Who'd make his way into the woods to find anyone here?"

He smiled, sort of. "I'll always be sorry for being away when you needed me."

"What would you have done?" She eyed him, and there was more of his Cassie in her gaze. "He had a knife. I was grateful you weren't here. He might have killed you. He might have—and this is my worst nightmare about that night—he might have made you watch. When I dream about it, you are here, and he makes you watch and then he kills you in front of me." Tears slipped down her cheeks, streaking her cold, dry skin. "I'm humiliated, and I know how it feels to have no control over your body, but the worst thing would have been to lose you, too."

"Are you blind, Cassie? You did lose me. You threw me out. You threw me away."

A sob escaped her—as if she didn't know she was crying.

"I'm sorry." He knelt in front of her. "Please, I'm sorry. But I'm angry, too. I love you. I always have. I tried to make you believe, and you didn't want me. I have no right to be angry because you were raped, but I am. You ran away from me."

"I feel as though it just happened yesterday."

She dropped the afghan and it puddled on the hearth. With her arms around him, she planted her chin on his shoulder. "I thought I had to deal with the rape so I'd love Hope, but I just learned to love her. The rape—I never dealt with it. I can parrot the facts—rape is violence. But I was vulnerable, and I am vulnerable with you. You can hurt me, Van. You can destroy me."

"I won't." He kissed her cheek.

"No—I can't look at you. Let me finish. I love you. I came here to make love with you, to see if I can be your wife again because I'm asking you to take me back."

"I hear a condition in your voice."

"I'm not sure I can do it," she said. "Be a woman again, and you deserve a woman who can love you in every way."

"I deserve you. I love you. If you love me at all, we'll make the rest happen. Eventually." He pulled back and pressed his hands to either side of her face. "You don't have to prove anything."

"Yes, I do." She stood and pulled a packet from her back pocket. "Show me the bedroom."

"Cassie." He stared at her. With red, wet cheeks, her hair in clotted strands around her face and a runny nose, she was still the most beautiful sight he'd ever seen. "As attractive as your offer is, I'm not sure you're setting the right mood for a seduction."

"Mood?" She mopped her face and tried to smooth her hair. As if she could see herself, she dropped her hands to her sides. "We'll have to do without mood. Are you willing to try with me?"

He caught up and held her close. "I'm willing to seduce you." He kissed her, and her mouth met his, her eagerness not feigned. He knew her that well. His breathing was harsh as he lifted his head. "Or to hold you, if that's what you want in the end."

She walked to the stairs, her hand holding his. "What did you do to the bedroom?"

Renovations weren't terribly seductive, either. "I made it bigger and we have a bathroom whose windows will never steam up. We'd need a lot bigger water heater."

She laughed with tear-sodden reluctance, but his pulse hammered. She could laugh when she was offering herself like a sacrifice. Maybe they still stood a slight chance.

"We," she said. "I like that."

"Me, too."

At the top of the stairs, she hesitated. He waited, not breathing. At last she started down the hall, and he followed.

"One thing we're not counting on," he said.

She turned, flight already in her eyes.

"What if I can't make love to a woman who's forcing herself? Wait—this isn't hypothetical. It's totally personal. What if I can't make love to you because you're forcing yourself? This is a road map back to our old problem. I don't want to hurt you, but I sure as hell don't want you to assume I don't want you."

She shook her head. "I'll know if I can—" She broke off. "Talking so much is embarrassing."

"I can help you with that." They reached his room. His clothes on the floor and his bunched up sheets weren't any more inviting than Cassie's I'm-not-sure approach to a scene he'd rather have set with romance. "Sorry it's such a mess."

"Shut up." She pulled her sweater over her head, and her hair fell to her thin shoulders. With her heart beating so hard, her full, bare breasts trembled. He swallowed.

Maybe he couldn't do this.

"I can't undress you," she said. "Maybe next time."

The silence between them suggested, *if we have a next time.*

He took off his T-shirt. She backed up as if he'd suddenly grown taller.

"I'll stay right here," he said.

"For pity's sake." She took two steps that brought her nose level with his chest. "I'm going to need some help. Nothing fancy. Just remind me how it all goes."

He laughed. "Sorry," he said.

She grinned. "It's nice to hear." She reached for

the tie on his flannel pajama pants, but her fingers drifted away.

He didn't let her fade. He reached for the button on her jeans. She sucked in her belly and he dropped to his knees. When he kissed her, just beneath her navel, she cradled his head against her.

He locked his arms around her thighs.

"This is enough for now," he said.

"Not for me." Her fingers in his hair made him shiver.

After a second, he pulled her zipper down. She trembled, but she didn't move as he slid his hands inside her jeans and pulled them down.

"I'm cold, Van."

"The house is drafty." Better if they both tried to believe she was cold because of the temperature. He picked her up, something she'd never allowed him to do because she'd been sensitive about being petite.

If she'd been a larger woman, maybe she'd have been better able to fight that guy off. He shook his head above her, glad she'd closed her eyes.

Gently, he laid her on his bed and stripped himself before he lay down beside her, pulling the sheets over them.

She turned into his arms. Her breasts teased his chest. His mouth went dry. She wrapped her leg around his.

"You're warm," she said.

"Yeah." His raspy voice startled him. Five years was a long time to love a woman, want her and believe he might never touch her again. Now he just had to make sure he didn't frighten her.

He tried to roll over and reach for the lamp. She tightened her arms.

"I want it on," she said.

"You sure?"

She kissed his chest, tracing his breastbone with her lips. Maybe she nodded, too. He couldn't tell. And he didn't care.

Her mouth reached his nipple, already hard with desire, like every inch of his body. Her mouth, moist and hot, made him groan, and he half expected her to leap out of bed.

But she smiled. Her lips curved around him, and his body took over.

He slid her beneath him, running his hands down her sides, finding curves he'd cherished, finding welcome he wasn't sure she'd still feel seconds from now.

He caught her nipple. She stiffened. Her heart beat so hard, she pulsed in his mouth. Her life was tied to his. He'd belonged to her before he'd ever known what love was. She was more precious to him than his own life.

As he splayed his fingers across her other breast, moaning again as her nipple rubbed his palm, she twined her legs around him again.

She threw back her head. He knew how she liked being touched. He followed the curve of her breasts with his mouth, open, wanting, needing until she curled into him so that he reached her nipple again. He reached between them and caressed her until she arched in his arms, crying out his name.

His name. Not in fear, not in anger. In wonder and the sheer relief of being sated. He knew the sounds she made when she made love.

"Now," she said. "Can you—"

"I don't have to. Isn't this enough for now?" Shaking in her arms, wanting her so much he was clinging to his own need with a slender, breaking thread of control, he was still afraid that taking her would make him lose her.

"If you don't, I might die."

"Oh." He lifted himself above her. Eyes half-closed, her body still moving, thrusting against him, she reminded him they were in this together. Not just this bed, but this life. "Where's the—"

"Find it. Please." She pushed her hair away from her face, her hands moving slowly as if she were touching herself in more intimate ways.

He stared, mesmerized. Her hands slid down her throat.

"Van."

He found the packet on the floor and tore it

open so urgently, he half feared he'd ripped the condom, too.

"Van."

"I have to make sure I didn't tear it."

"Van, now."

She held out her arms, and he was in them. Her hands slid all the way to his hips. She caught him between her palms and he thought he might die.

She opened her eyes wide. "Look at me," she said.

He wanted to look away as she helped him inside. His need was too much. His love, too intense.

She opened his mouth with hers. "I love you," she said against him.

He moved then because he couldn't stop himself. He forgot to be gentle, forgot everything except loving her, wanting her with him like this.

She felt tighter. He mourned the lost years, for her as well as for him, but he couldn't hold back. He drove the memories from his own head and shut the damn door on them. Never again would the past come between him and Cassie.

"I love you," he said over and over. Her incoherent, breathy cries robbed him of his last vestige of control. When her body pulsed around him, he was lost. He rose above her, grasped her hips and gave himself up.

What had she been afraid of? A woman's body was so subtle she could have hidden her response if she'd tried. He could hide nothing. He melted into her with the gratitude of finding lost love, and he felt so naked he couldn't speak.

MINUTES PASSED. They didn't move. Cassie smiled against his chest as he grew hard inside her again. He wanted her. Why had she ever doubted?

"Cass?"

"Hmm?" She kissed him, loving the scent and the taste of his skin.

"I think you can do it."

"I was just thinking the same about you."

"Did you bring more than one condom?"

"I'm sorry." She stroked his back. This man, virile and gentle, and all male, belonged to her. And she belonged to him. "I'm tempted to say it doesn't matter."

"It does." He pulled away, reluctance in his slow withdrawal, in the sigh of his breath. "We need time together with Hope before we add to our family."

"You do love her?" As he lay on his back, she lifted herself above him. "You're not just taking her on because of me?"

He twisted a strand of her hair. "That day, with Barr's kid—she stopped being yours. I forgot about that bastard who hurt you. She was just mine, my child to protect. Imagine, wanting to make a little boy pay for his parents' gossip. But the idea that someone could hurt Hope…"

"I know." She kissed him. "Being a parent is tricky business, huh?"

He nudged her elbow off his chest and caught her in a delicious kiss that put even Hope out of her mind. As his hand cupped her breast, she caught his wrist.

"What time is it?"

"Why?" His hand, sure and tender, made her dizzy. She seemed to be all nerve endings.

"We could go to my house," she said, "I need to be home when Hope wakes up."

"Maybe we could stop along the way."

"My thoughts, too."

He looked in her eyes, his own hollow with desire. Need swam through her veins. Her body— her soul—belonged to him. She recognized her mate.

AS DARK BLUE CREPT into the black sky, they showered together at Cassie's house. Even without closing his eyes all night, Van felt more awake than he had in five years. He handed Cassie a lacy camisole she'd dropped on the bed, thinking how much he'd enjoy peeling it off her later.

She pulled it over her head. "Are you sure about all this?"

"What?" He buttoned his shirt. "Not that I'm bothered if you're having second thoughts, because they're not about anything real."

She put on a sweater with a V-neck that dipped low enough to expose her camisole. The shadow of her skin beneath the lace fascinated him.

"Look at me," she said. "I mean, look at my face."

"For now." He kissed her forehead. "What's up, Cass?"

"When we walk out of this room, we're saying something to my father and Hope."

"Everything I want to say." He put on his jeans. "That I want to marry you again and I want to be Hope's father." He shook his head. "And Leo's son, though I may have failed him more than anyone."

"Dad should have told us something was wrong. I should have stayed in touch." She leaned down to kiss him as he bent for his shoes. He rubbed his cheek, liking the warmth of her lips. "Today isn't a time for recriminations."

"You're not bolting at the mention of marriage."

She sat on the bed as if her legs had given way. "Yeah," she said. "Funny enough, we're giving each other everything I want."

A knock at the door made them stare at each other.

"Cass," her father said, "time to get up. We have to make cocoa for Hope when she gets up."

"Tradition." Cassie stood, her eyes a little wary.

At last Van felt sure when he put his arm around her waist. "Here goes," he said. "I don't think your dad will mind."

"But what if you change your mind?"

"About the time the earth starts revolving backward," he said, and opened the door.

Leo's mouth dropped open. He shut it. "Van."

"Morning. I should have asked you before I stayed the night, but Cass and I got home in the early hours."

"She's your wife," Leo said.

"Not yet, but she will be again soon."

Down the hall, another door opened, and Hope burst out. "Santa," she said, dancing. Then she saw Van and she stopped dead.

"Hey," he said, lowering his voice, hoping she wouldn't be upset when she realized.

"He's real." She pressed her palms together, linking her fingers so tightly the tips turned white.

"Who's real, baby?" Cassie went to her first, but Hope ran around her, flinging herself into Van's open arms.

"Santa's real." She locked her arms like a vise around his neck. "Josh Barr told me Mommy was my Santa, but we saw Santa at the mall, and I asked him for you, Mr. Van, and here you are. He's really real."

Van held on tight. How long had she been his

daughter already? Before he'd even known. "You'd better believe."

He couldn't see for sure through his own tears, but he thought Cassie and Leo might be crying, too.

EPILOGUE

LAST ON THE JUDGE'S DOCKET, they waited until afternoon turned to an early January evening. Cassie held a wriggling Hope. Leo snoozed, jolting every so often when he woke himself snoring. Van just held her hand and looked like a man in a maternity waiting room.

"Are you worried?" she finally asked.

"I'm scared out of my wits. What if I'm a bad father?"

"Every parent feels that way."

"Can I call you Daddy now?" Hope asked. "I don't care what some man says, and it's taking too long."

Van glanced at Cassie. She'd thought waiting for the actual adoption would make calling Van Daddy more special for Hope. "Go ahead," she said. "We can't get any closer, and Van couldn't be more your father."

"I know that." Hope bounced again. "Why does some guy have to tell us it's okay?"

"That's the way it works," Van said. They'd

agreed to wait until Hope asked for the truth to give it. Her teenage years weren't that far away. "Why don't you give Mommy a rest and sit with me?"

"Okay, Daddy." She hopped on his lap, and the door opened to the judge's chambers.

His clerk beckoned them. "Sorry we've been so long. We're still dealing with cases from the New Year's Eve roadblocks. A small-town judge…"

Cassie barely understood what the woman was saying. Judge Jake Sloane rose from behind his desk, younger than she'd expected.

"I think we have all the paperwork in order." He held out his hand to Hope. "You must be Miss Warne."

Clinging to Van's hand, she looked up. "I thought I was going to be Hope Haddon."

"In a few minutes," he said.

Cassie tried to breathe. Their wedding next week couldn't be more stressful. She loved Van with no doubts whatsoever, but she'd been Hope's only parent for a long time.

"We don't really have a ceremony," Judge Sloane said. "Mrs. Haddon, will you step over here?"

She moved to Hope's side. "I'm still Cassie Warne until next week. If the name matters."

"Next week?"

"The wedding," Van said. "We wanted to do this first so Hope knows she's my daughter, no matter what."

"Okay." Judge Sloane didn't understand, but there were no rules against an adoption before a wedding. "Mr. Haddon, do you want to be Miss Warne's father from now on?"

"For good," Hope said, as if it were a test.

"For good and bad and everything else," he said. "How about you? Do you want to be my daughter?"

"I already am." Hope didn't seem to feel the portent of the moment. "Mommy—" she grabbed Cassie's hand "—are we all married together now?"

The judge shrugged, the shoulders of his robe looking awfully wide. "As married together as I've ever seen a family."

Cassie hugged Van, loving the strength of his body as he instinctively leaned into her. She lifted Hope between them. "We recognized each other all by ourselves—a husband, a wife, and our own little girl. How lucky are we?"

"Luck has nothing to do with being smart enough to grab love and never let go of it again," Van said. "Like I'm hanging onto you two."

"Uh-oh. Grampa's still asleep in the hall." Hope wriggled to get down, and Cassie shared a stunned glance with Van. They'd marched in, the three of them, alone. Hope tugged at the judge's voluminous sleeve. "We gotta start over, Mr. Judge, or he's gonna be ma-a-d. This was his idea. Him and me talked about it before Mommy and Daddy knew anything."

* * * * *

Welcome to cowboy country...

Turn the page for a sneak preview of
TEXAS BABY
by
Kathleen O'Brien
An exciting new title from
Harlequin Superromance for everyone
who loves stories about the West.

Harlequin Superromance—
Where life and love weave together in
emotional and unforgettable ways.

CHAPTER ONE

CHASE TRANSFERRED his gaze to the road and iden-
tified a foreign spot on the horizon. A car. Almost
half a mile away, where the straight, tree-lined
drive met the public road. He could tell it was
coming too fast, but judging the speed of a vehicle
moving straight toward you was tricky.

It wasn't until it was about two hundred yards
away that he realized the driver must be drunk…
or crazy. Or both.

The guy was going maybe sixty. On a private
drive, out here in ranch country, where kids or
horses or tractors or stupid chickens might come
darting out any minute, that was criminal. Chase
straightened from his comfortable slouch and
waved his hands.

"Slow down, you fool," he called out. He took
the porch steps quickly and began walking fast
down the driveway.

The car veered oddly, from one lane to another,
then up onto the slight rise of the thick green
spring grass. It just barely missed the fence.

"Slow down, damn it!"

He couldn't see the driver, and he didn't recognize this automobile. It was small and old, and couldn't have cost much even when it was new. It was probably white, but now it needed either a wash or a new paint job or both.

"Damn it, what's wrong with you?"

At the last minute, he had to jump away, because the idiot behind the wheel clearly wasn't going to turn to avoid a collision. He couldn't believe it. The car kept coming, finally slowing a little, but it was too late.

Still going about thirty miles an hour, it slammed into the large, white-brick pillar that marked the front boundaries of the house. The pillar wasn't going to give an inch, so the car had to. The front end folded up like a paper fan.

It seemed to take forever for the car to settle, as if the trauma happened in slow motion, reverberating from the front to the back of the car in ripples of destruction. The front windshield suddenly seemed to ice over with lethal bits of glassy frost. Then the side windows exploded.

The front driver's door wrenched open, as if the car wanted to expel its contents. Metal buckled hideously. Small pieces, like hubcaps and mirrors, skipped and ricocheted insanely across the oyster-shell driveway.

Finally, everything was still. Into the silence,

a plume of steam shot up like a geyser, smelling of rust and heat. Its snakelike hiss almost smothered the low, agonized moan of the driver.

Chase's anger had disappeared. He didn't feel anything but a dull sense of disbelief. Things like this didn't happen in real life. Not in his life. Maybe the sun had actually put him to sleep….

But he was already kneeling beside the car. The driver was a woman. The frosty glass-ice of the windshield was dotted with small flecks of blood. She must have hit it with her head, because just below her hairline a red liquid was seeping out. He touched it. He tried to wipe it away before it reached her eyebrow, though, of course, that made no sense at all. Her eyes were shut.

Was she conscious? Did he dare move her? Her dress was covered in glass, and the metal of the car was sticking out lethally in all the wrong places.

Then he remembered, with an intense relief, that every good medical man in the county was here, just behind the house, drinking his champagne. He found his phone and paged Trent.

The woman moaned.

Alive, then. Thank God for that.

He saw Trent coming toward him, starting out at a lope, but quickly switching to a full run.

"Get Dr. Marchant," Chase called. "Don't bother with 911."

Trent didn't take long to assess the situation.

A fraction of a second, and he began pulling out his cell phone and running toward the house.

The yelling seemed to have roused the woman. She opened her eyes. They were blue and clouded with pain and confusion.

"Chase," she said.

His breath stalled. His head pulled back. "What?"

Her only answer was another moan, and he wondered if he had imagined the word. He reached around her and put his arm behind her shoulders. She was tiny. Probably petite by nature, but surely way too thin. He could feel her shoulder blades pushing against her skin, as fragile as the wishbone in a turkey.

She seemed to have passed out, so he put his other arm under her knees and lifted her out. He tried to avoid the jagged metal, but her skirt caught on a piece and the tearing sound seemed to wake her again.

"No," she said. "Please."

"I'm just trying to help," he said. "It's going to be all right."

She seemed profoundly distressed. She wriggled in his arms, and she was so weak, like a broken bird. It made him feel too big and brutish. And intrusive. As if touching her this way, his bare hands against the warm skin behind her knees, were somehow a transgression.

He wished he could be more delicate. But he smelled gasoline, and he knew it wasn't safe to leave her here.

Finally he heard the sound of voices, as guests began to run around the side of the house, alerted by Trent. Dr. Marchant was at the front, racing toward them as if he were forty instead of seventy. Susannah was right behind him, her green dress floating around her trim legs.

"Please," the woman in his arms murmured again. She looked at him, the expression in her blue eyes lost and bewildered. He wondered if she might be on drugs. Hitting her head on the windshield might account for this unfocused, glazed look, but it couldn't explain the crazy driving.

"Please, put me down. Susannah… The wedding…"

Chase's arms tightened instinctively, and he froze in his tracks. She whimpered, and he realized he might be hurting her. "Say that again?"

"The wedding. I have to stop it."

* * * * *

Be sure to look for TEXAS BABY,
available September 11, 2007,
as well as other fantastic Superromance titles
available in September.

HARLEQUIN® *Super Romance*®

Welcome to Cowboy Country...

TEXAS BABY

by *Kathleen O'Brien*

#1441

Chase Clayton doesn't know what to think.
A beautiful stranger has just crashed his
engagement party, demanding that he not
marry because she's pregnant with his baby.
But the kicker is—he's never seen her before.

Look for TEXAS BABY and other fantastic
Superromance titles on sale September 2007.

Available wherever books are sold.

HARLEQUIN® *Super Romance*®

**Where life and love weave together
in emotional and unforgettable ways.**

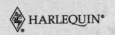

EVERLASTING LOVE™

Every great love has a story to tell ™

Third time's a charm.

Texas summers. Charlie Morrison.
Jasmine Boudreaux has always connected
the two. Her relationship with Charlie
begins and ends in high school. Twenty
years later it begins again—and ends again.
Now fate has stepped in one more time—
will Jazzy and Charlie finally give in to
the love they've shared all this time?

Look for

Summer After Summer
by
Ann DeFee

**Available September
wherever books are sold.**

REQUEST YOUR FREE BOOKS!
2 FREE NOVELS PLUS 2 FREE GIFTS!

HARLEQUIN®

Super Romance®

Exciting, emotional, unexpected!

The latest novel in The Lakeshore Chronicles
by *New York Times* bestselling author

SUSAN WIGGS

From the award-winning author of *Summer at Willow Lake*
comes an unforgettable story of a woman's emotional journey
from the heartache of the past to hope for the future.

With her daughter grown and flown, Nina Romano is ready to
embark on a new adventure. She's waited a long time for dating,
travel and chasing dreams. But just as she's beginning to enjoy
being on her own, she finds herself falling for Greg Bellamy,
owner of the charming Inn at Willow Lake and a single father
with two kids of her own.

DOCKSIDE

"The perfect summer read." —Debbie Macomber

Available the first week of August 2007
wherever paperbacks are sold!

MIRA®

www.MIRABooks.com

MSW2475

ATHENA FORCE

Heart-pounding romance and thrilling adventure.

Professional negotiator Lindsey Novak is faced with her biggest challenge—to buy back Teal Arnett, a young woman with unique powers. In the process Lindsey uncovers a devastating plot that involves scientists from around the globe, and all of them lead to one woman who is bent on destroying Athena Academy…at any cost.

LOOK FOR

THE GOOD THIEF

by Judith Leon

Available September wherever you buy books.